To Turning Thirty!
To Being Bad! To Us!

To Catherine . . . Who's been coasting too long on **Still Waters.** Introverted, shy, yet untouchably luminous, she's a real Grace Kelly. But she always puts business before pleasure. Then she catches the scent of a delicious male acquaintance who sparks her fantasy: to be treated like a princess—with a worshipping commoner who'll do precisely what he's told.

To Kallie . . . A talented artist, she's been putting off the one thing she's been needing for so long—a hot, no-strings-attached man whose attraction is purely **Skin Deep.** Now that she's found him— tousled hair, blue eyes, and a killer smile—she's making good on her bet. What she wants is a go-all-the-way, no-holds-barred fling that'll take her into thirty and beyond. What she gets is a surprise.

To Gina . . . A former **Party Girl,** a little jaded, burned once too often, still a little reckless, and a strict nonbeliever in love. Until a getaway cruise leads to a head-on collision with the man who broke her heart years ago. He was so sexy, so perfect, so typically male. Now he's back. This is going to be one risky bet. But Gina still wants him—in the worst way. . . .

Play with Me

Janice Maynard

A SIGNET ECLIPSE BOOK

SIGNET ECLIPSE
Published by New American Library, a division of
Penguin Group (USA) Inc., 375 Hudson Street,
New York, New York 10014, USA
Penguin Group (Canada), 90 Eglinton Avenue East, Suite 700, Toronto,
Ontario M4P 2Y3, Canada (a division of Pearson Penguin Canada Inc.)
Penguin Books Ltd., 80 Strand, London WC2R 0RL, England
Penguin Ireland, 25 St. Stephen's Green, Dublin 2,
Ireland (a division of Penguin Books Ltd.)
Penguin Group (Australia), 250 Camberwell Road, Camberwell, Victoria 3124,
Australia (a division of Pearson Australia Group Pty. Ltd.)
Penguin Books India Pvt. Ltd., 11 Community Centre, Panchsheel Park,
New Delhi - 110 017, India
Penguin Group (NZ), cnr Airborne and Rosedale Roads, Albany,
Auckland 1310, New Zealand (a division of Pearson New Zealand Ltd.)
Penguin Books (South Africa) (Pty.) Ltd., 24 Sturdee Avenue,
Rosebank, Johannesburg 2196, South Africa

Penguin Books Ltd., Registered Offices: 80 Strand, London WC2R 0RL, England

First published by Signet Eclipse, an imprint of New American Library,
a division of Penguin Group (USA) Inc.

First Printing, January 2007
10 9 8 7 6 5 4 3 2 1

SIGNET ECLIPSE and logo are trademarks of Penguin Group (USA) Inc.

LIBRARY OF CONGRESS CATALOGING-IN-PUBLICATION DATA:
Maynard, Janice.
  Play with me / Janice Maynard.
      p. cm.
  ISBN-13: 978-0-451-22023-3
  ISBN-10: 0-451-22023-4
  I. Title.
  PS3613.A958P63 2007
  813'.6—dc22
                                    2006017835
Set in Berkeley
Designed by Spring Hoteling

Printed in the United States of America

PUBLISHER'S NOTE
This is a work of fiction. Names, characters, places, and incidents either are the product of the author's imagination or are used fictitiously, and any resemblance to actual persons, living or dead,
business establishments, events, or locales is entirely coincidental.
   The publisher does not have any control over and does not assume any responsibility for author
or third-party Web sites or their content.

For Charlie—husband, playmate, lover, friend.

Play with Me

Prologue

At a simple wrought-iron table in the garden of one of Charleston's finest restaurants, three beautiful women each lifted a glass of champagne.

"To us." The words were uttered in unison. The synchronism was not unusual. They had known one another since kindergarten.

The redhead, the only extrovert in the group, eyed her companions. "So . . . we're agreed, then."

The cool blonde, looking nervous, licked her lips. She had consumed more alcohol than usual, and she was afraid her judgment might be the teensiest bit impaired. "What if we can't go through with it?"

The petite brunette, her ringless fingers restlessly twisting the stem of her glass, nibbled her bottom lip. "We don't have a choice. We've made a pact. As of today, April first."

The redhead had lush curves that strained the bodice of her dress. She took another reckless sip and grinned. "Damned straight. And if either of you two wimp out, I'll harass you unmercifully. We're going to be thirty in twelve months, ladies. *Thirty.*" Her face sobered, and she sat back in her chair.

The blonde nodded slowly. "You're right. I know you're right. But every time I think about it, I feel faint."

The little brunette stretched a leg beneath the table, feeling around for her sandal. "At least you know your scenario is possible," she muttered. "Mine has the potential to blow up in my face and ruin something really good."

The redhead, ignoring such obvious negative thoughts, signaled the waiter for their check. "The die is cast, my friends. We each have a year to make one of our deepest, naughtiest fantasies come true. And when the big 3-0 rolls around, we'll be back here to share all the juicy details."

Still Waters

One

Catherine Maderis slipped on a pair of cotton gloves and reverently lifted the sheet of parchment paper from its specially designed case. It was a bill of lading from a shipping company that had operated in Charleston during the late 1700s. The handwriting was spidery but legible, and the mundane list of supplies made her pulse race.

The museum had acquired this document and others from a recent estate sale. As the full-time archivist, it was her job to examine, catalog, and preserve the unexpected treasure trove.

When she next looked up from her work several hours later, her growling stomach reminded her it was time for lunch. She forced herself to take a break and munch on an apple. It was not unusual for her to lose track of time. She loved her job.

Although she had learned to cope with her innate shyness, dealing with books and papers was far more appealing than any type of employment where she would have had to deal with the public every day. With a degree in library science and some specialized training, she'd snagged this job five years ago, and she enjoyed it more every day.

As a pale, skinny, blond-haired child, her severe stuttering had made her an object of ridicule. Intensive speech therapy and some counseling enabled her to overcome her affliction, but those years had left their mark. She preferred to stay out of the limelight, and she thrived on peace and quiet.

Her parents were in their late forties when she was born. Her unwelcome and unexpected advent into their lives momentarily disrupted their calm, orderly routine. But as wealthy and influential Charlestonians, they were able to afford a series of well-trained nannies and prestigious schools.

Catherine spent little time with her parents as she grew up. They were distant, almost strangers. As a young adult she had tried to win their affection, but it was a dismal, esteem-shattering task. They passed away two years ago within months of each other, bequeathing to Catherine a historic and exquisitely maintained "single" house and an embarrassing amount of money.

She tossed her apple core into the trash can and eyed the phone. Ever since dinner three nights ago with Kallie and Gina, her stomach had been doing flip-flops. Definitely too much wine and not enough sense. Birthdays were no reason to panic. So they were twenty-nine, so what?

All of their birthdays actually fell within one five-day

span in early April, hence the recent celebratory meal. They had met as five-year-olds in elementary school, and the happy accident of having almost identical birthdays had cemented the blossoming friendships. Now, with Catherine's parents gone, Kallie and Gina were the closest thing to family she could claim.

But although they loved her dearly, they weren't likely to let her out of this crazy pact. Gina, in particular. Gina was always pushing Catherine to get out and meet men. Gina knew about the shyness and the childhood trauma, of course. Gina had been the one, in many cases, protecting Catherine from the worst of the teasing and name-calling. One painful day, Gina even took her fists to a mean, taunting bully twice her size. But the kid hadn't been a match for a furious redhead whose best friend was crying hysterically. Gina had beaten the crap out of the boy. Even though it meant a week in detention.

Gina had a heart for the underdog, even in those days. But her sympathy was laced with tough love. It wouldn't matter to her that Catherine's legs were shaky and her heart was pounding. Gina would tell her to suck it up and be a big girl.

So backing out was not an option.

Catherine wondered if her two friends had made any kind of start on the whole hidden-fantasy challenge. Gina was a workaholic, so probably not. Her passion for Charleston's charity work was evident in her single-minded devotion to her many hours of volunteer service on nonprofit boards. And Kallie was a renowned procrastinator. She had an artist's temperament, and when she was painting, she could go days without surfacing.

Which left Catherine. Catherine who was a firm proponent of getting unpleasant tasks out of the way so they wouldn't hang over her head.

Not that Phillip Trent fell under the category of unpleasant. Far from it. But to pursue her hidden fantasy, she would have to push past her comfort zone and venture into uncharted waters. Dread and anticipation were odd and unsettling companions.

She picked up the phone and inhaled. She had jotted down Phillip's number in her neat handwriting on a sticky note. She punched in four digits and then slammed down the receiver, her hand shaking. She couldn't do this over the phone. It would be face-to-face, or nothing.

She glanced at the clock on the wall. She had already put in her allotted hours this week, and her schedule was flexible. Since she darned sure wasn't going to show up at Phillip's house, she'd have to go to his office. It wasn't an ideal plan, but it was the best she could do at the moment.

She made a quick trip to the ladies' room to tidy up. As she dressed that morning, she'd had Phillip in the back of her mind. The simple periwinkle silk dress she wore had a wrap bodice and a narrow skirt. It was plain enough to wear to work, but the beauty and luster of the fabric shored up her waning confidence.

She elected to walk the four blocks to Phillip's office.

Her low-heeled pumps were comfortable, and the weather was just about perfect. Spring in Charleston was a treat for the senses.

Phillip's business occupied an old house that had been lovingly restored. At first glance, a high-rise of steel and concrete seemed more his style, but she didn't really know him all that well. They moved in the same social circles and had mutual friends, but that was about it. For the last couple of years they'd engaged in friendly conversation from time to time. He was wildly attractive and way out of her league, but she couldn't seem to get past her helpless fascination with him. Though his sheer size and physical presence intimidated her, she wished fervently that she was the kind of woman who could tame such an unapologetically alpha male.

He was a shark in the business world, a developer who had his fingers in so many pies it was a wonder he had time to sleep.

For a brief moment her mind skittered off in another direction. Phillip in bed. Phillip nude. Phillip's broad shoulders and golden skin just begging to be touched.

She paused on the street corner and took a bottle of water from her purse. Her throat was dry, and the pleasant spring day seemed suddenly too warm. After draining half the contents, she recapped the bottle and stood irresolute. The urge to flee was almost overpowering.

In very stressful situations her stutter had been known to recur. She would be mortified if it happened with Phillip.

Deep breaths. Calm thoughts. She focused on the image of thirty candles on a birthday cake. Some of her panic receded, and she lifted her chin. She would *not* chicken out.

A discreet, polished brass sign identified TRENT ENTER-PRISES. But for that one anomaly, the building seemed like an attractive private home, it's neatly manicured walk bordered by pink and white azaleas.

She rang the buzzer and heard a click as the security lock was released. Inside, a smiling secretary seated at an antique cherry table greeted her. Unfortunately, though the young woman was charming and friendly, she was also fiercely protective of her boss's time.

"I'm terribly sorry, ma'am. Mr. Trent's schedule today is a bear. He's had back-to-back appointments, and now he's on a transatlantic conference call. Would you like to make an appointment? He could do two o'clock tomorrow."

Catherine felt her neck flush. If she left, she might never return. But she didn't seem to have many choices. "No. Thank you. Perhaps I'll call and arrange something later. Thank you for your time."

Embarrassed and humiliated for no substantial reason, she edged back out the door and fled.

Halfway down the street, a shout stopped her in her tracks. She turned around and saw Phillip Trent jogging in her direction, a look of urgency on his face. When he caught up with her, his forehead was damp with perspiration. His expensive suit was rumpled, his crisp white dress shirt was wilting, and his shoes were covered in dust from some nearby street construction.

Another man might have looked ridiculous. Phillip Trent looked attractive even with disheveled hair and his tie askew. Perhaps more so.

He was a big man. Big all over. Broad-shouldered, several inches over six feet, a couple hundred pounds of firm, toned muscle. She'd seen him stripped to the waist on one memorable occasion in the midst of a sailing regatta. The image returned to steal her breath and tighten her nipples.

She licked her lips. "Phillip. What are you doing?"

He grimaced and ran a hand through his hair, making the disarray even worse. He jerked his tie loose and stuffed it in his pocket. "Why the hell couldn't you have waited a few minutes?"

Her eyes narrowed. "I wasn't given that choice. I was told that the great and powerful Oz couldn't be disturbed."

Her sarcasm made him grin, and she saw the strain and disgruntlement melt from his face. "Belinda takes her job very seriously. It's been a hell of a day, and I can't really blame her. But if you had told her who you were, she'd have brought you in to see me, regardless."

Catherine frowned. "Why?"

He shrugged, and a hot look flashed in his eyes and disappeared, leaving his usual steady smile in place. "Because, on the off chance you ever stopped by for some business advice, I wanted to be notified ASAP."

"Oh." What he wasn't saying made her giddy.

He touched her cheek. "Is that why you came to see me, Catherine? For business advice?"

His fingers felt like sunburn on her skin. "No." His

11

closeness reduced her to monosyllabic responses. But at least she wasn't stuttering.

He grinned. "Too bad. I was hoping you wanted to sell me that fabulous house of yours."

His teasing relaxed her a bit. "In your dreams." It had been a running joke since the first time they met.

His thumb moved back and forth over her cheekbone. "Then why, Catherine?"

Her courage failed her. "It was nothing important," she said lightly, lying through her teeth. "Just a whim. I was in the neighborhood and thought I'd see where you work. I'm sorry I bothered you."

He took both her hands, his expression serious. "Listen, honey. Don't blow me off. Why did you come?" An alarm on his watch beeped, and he glanced down at his wrist with a curse.

She tried to tug her hands free, but he wasn't budging. His expression was equal parts harassed and desperate.

He gripped more tightly, threatening to crack her fingers. "Tonight," he said simply, stubbornness written all over his face. "I'll pick you up for dinner at seven. We'll continue this conversation."

"But I—"

He cut her off with a fierce frown. "Do you have other plans?"

"No, but—"

"Then be ready."

He brushed a kiss on her hot cheek and released her, turning abruptly to jog back down the street.

Phillip reknotted his tie as he ran. He slipped in the back door to his office, meeting his disgruntled secretary with a placating grin.

She made hand gestures toward the lobby. "He's been sitting out there for twenty minutes. I can only be so entertaining without a raise."

He chucked her chin. "Don't get sassy. Give me three minutes and show him in."

Phillip ducked into his private bathroom, ran a wet cloth over his face, and returned to his desk, locating the necessary file just as a distinguished-looking older man walked through the door.

It took a bit of ass-kissing and some serious groveling, but he smoothed the client's ruffled feathers and managed to look suitably penitent for keeping him waiting. All in all, a damned fine performance, especially considering he wanted to consign the guy to the devil and drag Catherine back by the hair.

It had been pure chance that he'd glanced out his window and saw her leaving the premises. His abrupt end to the conference call had been just short of rude, and the sprint that followed had been spurred by a sense of urgency.

Remembering the feel of Catherine's skin made his breath come faster. He clenched his fist on the desk and produced what he hoped was an interested smile. The old geezer was droning on, but since he owned a sizeable empty building just north of Rainbow Row, Phillip was forced to listen to his proposal.

When the meeting finally drew to a close, it was all Phillip could do not to shout with relief. Belinda escorted their client to the door and then left promptly at five, leaving Phillip to collapse in his leather executive chair. He spun around aimlessly like a kid with nothing to do but enjoy the moment.

His mind flitted off in a dozen directions. Catherine had come to see him. Voluntarily. Hot damn. There might be a breach in the castle walls after all.

For a three-month period last year he had pursued her hard and fast. He lost track of the number of times he had asked her out. But in every instance, she had turned him down. Politely. Charmingly. Apologetically. Even sweetly. But rejection, nevertheless.

He was a confident guy, but he wasn't stupid. And he liked to think he wasn't a jerk. She just wasn't into him. It was a bitter pill to swallow, but he'd taken his knocks like a man and backed away with some degree of dignity, even though it had hurt surprisingly much.

Catherine fascinated and attracted him more than any woman had in a long time . . . maybe ever. Her natural grace and cool elegance reminded him of a young Grace Kelly. And it wasn't much of a stretch to imagine Catherine as a movie star princess. Something about her stood out in a crowd. Although she never flaunted her looks and normally stayed at the fringes of a social gathering, her luminous beauty drew him like the proverbial moth to a flame.

And then there was his secret fetish. She wore pearls . . . all the time. He'd seen her in formal evening gowns with pearls. He'd seen her in neatly pressed capri pants and a T-shirt with pearls. And although he had yet to witness it, he would bet his last dollar that she looked damned amazing in a sexy white negligee with pearls. He had a number of really great fantasies that revolved around Catherine and those pearls.

He had resigned himself to having the fantasies and nothing more. The lady wasn't interested. Which left him awkward and wistful, two things not in his usual repertoire of reactions.

Around Catherine, his customary savoir faire evaporated, making him feel like a gawky adolescent. He had the power to manipulate powerful men and women into giving him what he wanted, be it companies or land. But one slender blonde had managed to keep Phillip Trent at arm's length with nothing more than a steady look.

He'd backed off when he realized she wasn't going to relent. No point in embarrassing them both. But he hadn't stopped looking. It was pathetic, but he could even describe a big chunk of her wardrobe in detail. There was one cherry red sweater she'd worn to a Christmas concert. The soft cashmere had clung to her breasts . . .

Whoa . . . he adjusted himself and stood up to pace restlessly. Why had she come to see him if not for business? Why had a woman who'd shut him down time again suddenly shown a modicum of interest?

His pulse was jerky, and his skin felt tight. If the princess in the castle had opened some kind of secret garden door, he sure as hell wasn't going to waste any time.

He'd wage an all-out assault, disguised, of course, in the impeccable and sophisticated manners of a quintessential southern gentleman.

At least until he made it through her bedroom door . . .

Catherine dithered over what to wear like a sixteen-year-old girl on prom night. Ideally, she needed something that advertised a possible seduction without looking slutty. Some women could do sexy/classy. She doubted she was one of them. She had three kinds of outfits. Business attire, comfortable/casual, and evening wear.

Nothing in any of those three categories screamed, "Take me, I'm yours." Nothing in her closet was the kind of clothing that advertised a woman's availability. Even her evening gowns were more sedate than sexy.

But maybe that was okay. What she was about to do tonight was merely setting the stage. And she was nervous enough without wearing clothes that might make her uncomfortable. When she was with Phillip this evening, she had to take the first step toward her hidden fantasy. It wasn't necessary to show skin at this stage in the game. She'd fortify her courage with the familiar, the comfortable.

When the doorbell rang at five till seven, she was ready. She exited the house, crossed the length of the front porch, and slipped through the door leading to the sidewalk. Her historic home sat at right angles to the street, and the property was enclosed by a tall privacy fence. If Phillip thought it strange that she didn't invite him in, he made no comment.

He was dressed in a different suit, and it was clear he

had been home to shower and shave. He was very dark, but there was no sign of a five o'clock shadow. His eyes gleamed as he assessed her black slacks and baby blue sweater set. She had on heels, but she still felt tiny standing beside him.

He took her hand. "You look beautiful, Catherine."

She smiled, feeling jittery and nervous and excited all at the same time. "Thank you."

On the ride over to the restaurant they made pleasant chitchat about the spring weather, but all the while she couldn't take her eyes off his hands and his firm grip on the wheel. She wondered if he was just as confident in bed. Somehow she had a feeling she knew the answer to that question.

Over shrimp Creole and garden salads they played a dance of unspoken words. She rarely flirted . . . she didn't really know how. But with Phillip she felt safe. It was odd, really, because he was not at all a safe kind of man. There was something untamed about him despite his hand-tailored clothing and easy elegance.

All the sophisticated polish in the world couldn't disguise the real essence of the male animal beneath the surface. He was kind on occasion, generous—she knew that from Gina—and he played fair in the business world. But when all was said and done, his forceful vitality made other men seem effeminate and weak.

He attracted her and intimidated her. In the past she had let her fears win out, but no more.

Over coffee he stripped off the gloves. "Why are you here, Catherine?"

She wasn't prepared for his bluntness, and she choked and sputtered.

He handed her a napkin. "I'm sorry I startled you, but the question still stands."

She dabbed her lips with the napkin and laid it on the table. She saw him take a glance at the trace of pink lipstick on the snowy white cloth.

She shrugged. "You invited me to dinner."

His eyes narrowed at her deliberate obtuseness. "You know what I mean. Why now?"

She cleared her throat. "I wanted to invite you to the museum's Midsummer Night's Masked Ball. April isn't summer, of course, but they liked the name. I have to attend, and I need an escort."

He sat back in his chair, his fingers steepled beneath his chin. His steady regard made her want to squirm in her seat. She resisted the urge . . . barely.

He lifted an eyebrow, his expression calculating. She had the sense he could see into every corner of her psyche, and it thrilled and scared her at the same time.

He finally sighed and reached forward to take a drink from his coffee cup. Replacing it in the saucer with a soft clink, he cocked his head. "I'm not settling for that answer, honey. I've asked you out repeatedly, and you shot me down time and again. You don't strike me as the kind of woman who enjoys being the pursuer. There has to be more to this."

Well, darn. She hadn't expected him to be so analytical.

She looked down at her lap and then back at him. Lord, the man was gorgeous. "There were reasons before . . . but things have changed."

Interest sharpened his gaze. "Like what? You had a secret husband you had to get rid of? You were a spy for the CIA? You were contemplating becoming a nun? Tell me, Catherine. The curiosity is killing me."

His droll humor made her laugh softly. "Nothing so dramatic."

"Then, what?"

She gathered her courage. "I've always thought you were a very attractive man."

"But, what?"

It was her turn to sigh. "I was scared of you."

He blinked in shock, and his expression was equal parts insulted and crestfallen. Then he sobered. "I'm sorry, Catherine," he said, his voice strangely formal. "I never should have kept pursuing you after the first couple of times you told me no. I apologize."

For a moment his eyes and his heart were wide open to her, and she saw the depths of his mortification. He had misunderstood completely, and she felt awful. Enough so that she reached across the table and took his hand, something she would never have dared to do in other circumstances.

She gripped his fingers tightly. "No, no, no," she said hastily. "That's not what I meant. I wasn't afraid you were stalking me. And I have to confess . . . it was flattering."

A bit of the darkness left his face, and his jaw un-
clenched. Puzzlement etched his expression. "Then, why?
Why wouldn't you go out with me?"

She released his hand and sat back, her teeth biting into
her bottom lip. She'd hoped he wouldn't press for reasons.
"You're big . . . and male."

He frowned. "Has someone hurt you, Catherine?" he
asked, his voice gentle.

God, this was hard. She wrinkled her nose. "No. I
promise. That's not it."

He sat quietly, waiting as though he had all the patience
in the world. And in his eyes she saw something that gave
her the courage to continue. "I've always been shy, Phillip.
As a child . . . well, let's just say that it was crippling. I've
come a long way, and of course I date and go out with men.
But you're different . . . you seem a little bit dangerous."

He slumped in his chair as if he had taken a punch to
the gut. "God, Catherine," he muttered. "If this is supposed
to be making me feel better, it's not working. I swear on
everything that's holy I would never lay a hand on you."

She was genuinely shocked. "Of course not. Don't be
ridiculous." Then she realized how her words had sounded.
She shook her head vehemently. "I didn't mean physically
dangerous." She could tell that her fumbling explanations
weren't making a bit of sense.

It was time to quit tiptoeing around the truth. She
gripped her hands in her lap, her back straight, her chin up.
"I was afraid of you sexually."

Two

Phillip couldn't have been more shocked if she'd confessed to being a serial killer. His mouth opened and closed, but no sound came out.

Catherine's face turned pink all over, and she looked anywhere but at him. Her hand went to her throat and toyed with her pearls. Just like that, he got hard. And it was damned difficult to conduct a rational conversation when every ounce of blood in his brain had headed south.

He swallowed and reached blindly for his water glass. His pretty princess looked like she might faint at any second. Perhaps it was time for him to salvage the situation.

He scrubbed a hand across his forehead. For a moment he wondered if he had heard her correctly. But nothing else sounded remotely similar. She was afraid of his sexuality. Didn't seem promising for him. But on the other hand, Catherine was here. That had to count for something.

He said her name softly. "Catherine."

She looked up at him, and the vulnerability in her eyes squeezed his heart.

He smiled at her, swamped by a wave of affection and something far more alarming. He ignored those unexplored feelings. They could wait. "You're afraid of me sexually? What does that mean?"

She shrugged, clearly uneasy. "You know all those times you asked me out? Every time I got close to you . . . physically, I mean . . . you made me feel things. You have this civilized veneer, but I could tell you're a man with strong appetites."

"And that scared you?"

She shook her head. Her eyes had darkened to indigo. "What scared me was how I reacted to you. I was afraid I would do something crazy."

He couldn't help the little grin he felt lifting the corners of his mouth. "And do you still feel those things?"

She nodded, looking for all the world like a naughty child. "Yes."

He tried to keep a serious face, but she was so damned cute. "I'm really happy to hear that. I don't like to be the only one suffering."

Now she finally looked straight at him, her eyes filled with faint shock and what was almost certainly pleased interest. "You suffered?"

She sounded happy.

His grin was bigger this time. "Yes, Catherine. I suffered. I wanted you desperately, and you had no interest in me at all. That's tough on a guy's ego."

"I was interested," she muttered.

"But . . ."

"But I was scared."

He drummed his fingers on the table. "So we're back to that. And are you scared now?"

Her back straightened another millimeter. "Yes." Her haughty inflection would have done any princess proud.

"And yet, here you are."

"I told you . . . there were reasons before. Things have changed."

"What things have changed?"

She wrinkled her nose. "I made a promise to some friends."

"About what?"

"About you."

"What about me?" He was intrigued, but Catherine had a stubborn look on her face.

She lifted her chin. "I'd rather not say. It's personal."

"If it's about me, don't you think I have a right to know?"

"No."

Her response was unequivocal, and he decided to let it rest for the moment. "Well, in that case, please tell me why you were afraid to ask me to take you to the ball. Surely you knew I would say yes. I made my interest blindingly clear."

"You could have changed your mind."

"It was just three months ago. Do you think I'm that shallow and fickle?"

"I thought you might have been mad at me. For turning you down."

He chuckled. "I promise you, hon. I'm not that poor a

sport. You could have turned me down a hundred times, and I still would have been interested in you."

"Oh."

He lifted his hand and summoned the waiter to bring their check. "How about we go back to your house?"

Alarm skittered across her expressive face, and she went pale.

He sighed. "For a nightcap and some conversation, Catherine. It's far too soon for anything else."

She frowned. "It is?"

"Yes," he said firmly, wondering if he was trying to convince her or himself.

They made the trip back to her house in silence. He found a parking spot not far from her door and came around the car to help her out. The scent of flowers hung in the night air, but all he could think about was getting close enough to Catherine to smell the unique fragrance of her soft skin.

Her hands shook as she tried to unlock the outer door. Finally, he took the key from her and, when they were both inside, locked the street entrance behind them.

He took a moment to peruse his surroundings. The famous Charleston design, a house only one room wide, was repeated many times in the city, but the Maderis property was an architectural gem. Because the family fortunes had never been depleted by gambling or financial reverses, the house had been kept in perfect condition. The small but private yard was immaculately landscaped. A gurgling fountain made tinkling music.

He followed Catherine up the steps to the front door,

and this time she was able to manage the lock herself. She led him from the foyer into a formal drawing room to the right and offered him a seat.

She looked as nervous as a cat facing a tub of bathwater.

He tried to appear as nonthreatening as possible, but it was no easy task, given that he wanted to devour her. Being a gentleman was a strain in certain situations.

Her hands twisted at her waist. "I'll pour us some wine."

She disappeared, and he stood up to examine the room. He was particularly interested in the pictures on the wall. There was an oil painting of a young girl, possibly Catherine. She didn't look very happy, and he wondered what her life had been like growing up in this houseful of priceless antiques.

When Catherine returned, he had finished giving himself a lecture. She was shy. She was skittish. She had come to him, and he wasn't going to mess this up.

Their fingers brushed when she handed him a glass. The hair on the back of his neck stood up, and he shivered. If he didn't get a taste of her mouth soon, he might go stark raving mad.

Fifteen minutes of pleasantries were all he could stand.

He stood up abruptly, placing his untouched drink on a pie-crust table. "May I have a tour?"

She nodded. "Of course."

The house was beautiful, but all he really cared about was seeing her bedroom. For some reason it seemed vitally important to study where she slept. He'd given the other rooms no more than a cursory glance from the doorway, so she must have been surprised when he entered her bedroom and stood near the fireplace.

He touched the mantel. "It still works? You haven't gone to gas logs?"

She smiled ruefully. "I love the fireplace. I have it inspected twice a year, and the insurance is exorbitant, but I can't give it up despite the fact that our cold weather season is so short."

He wandered around the room, examining knickknacks, studying artwork. The room was as elegant as the rest of the house, but with a subtle difference. The other areas were stiffly formal, as though they had been designed by a high-priced decorator. Catherine's boudoir was just as classy, but it was warm and inviting. Celadon with dashes of white and lemon yellow.

There were daisies in a crystal case on her dresser, and a handmade cloth baby doll reclined in the cherry rocker.

When he couldn't resist any longer, he stared at the bed. It was a carved rice bed swathed in mosquito netting, and it looked as romantic and provocative as any movie set. He raised an eyebrow.

Catherine was standing in the doorway to the hall as though afraid to get close to him. He bit the inside of his cheek to keep from smiling. "I like it," he said softly. "It looks like you."

"Like me?" A little crease appeared between her brows.

He nodded. "Feminine, classy, and damned sexy."

"I don't really need the netting," she confessed with a guilty grin. "There are never bugs in the house."

He stared at the bed, the plump pillows, the thick fluffy embroidered comforter, white on white. He imagined Catherine dropping her nightgown to the floor, slipping bare-skinned between the sheets, twitching the netting closed with a slender hand.

He cleared his throat. "I do like it," he said, his voice gruff. His control was raveling. "Perhaps you could show me the garden now."

Outside he took several gulps of the sweet night air. The humidity was low, and the gentle breeze felt icy cold against his overheated skin.

He followed Catherine to a bench near the fountain. It wasn't very wide, and once seated, they were pressed almost hip to hip. He shrugged out of his jacket and laid it across his lap. Moments later he rolled up his sleeves. He was burning up, and he wondered if he had a fever.

Catherine's head was bent slightly so that a fall of hair obscured her expression. Her palms rested on the bench, and the hand closest to him brushed his thigh ever so slightly. *Sweet God almighty.*

A great shudder worked through his frame. He gritted his teeth against a powerful arousal so strong it threatened to wrench him apart. He didn't know what to do, and that indecision shook him. He was afraid if he made one wrong step, she would bolt, and this fragile chink in the castle wall would be closed to him forever.

Then his heart stopped when a small, soft hand tentatively spanned the tiny distance between them and claimed his knee.

To his everlasting embarrassment, he almost whimpered. Almost, but not quite. Instead, he went perfectly still. She had to have noticed. Even his heart quit beating. He was sure of it.

Perhaps his total lack of reaction bothered her, because she made a little sound of distress and tried to remove her hand.

"No," he said hoarsely. "Keep it there." His big hand covered hers, trapping it against his leg.

He heard and felt her sigh.

Her voice was little more than a whisper. "I'm sorry, Phillip. I'm really not very good at this."

He turned and scooped her into his lap, ignoring her halfhearted protest and his jacket that tumbled to the ground. He held her close to his chest. Just held her. Her hair tickled his chin.

His heart slammed against his ribs. This chaste embrace with Catherine was more arousing than any full-fledged sexual encounter in recent memory. Not to mention the fact that he had been celibate for at least four months.

At thirty-five he had almost given up on casual sex. It invariably left him feeling empty and depressed. And once he met Catherine and knew he wanted to make her his, he had lost all interest in other women.

He pressed his lips to the crown of her head. "You feel good in my arms," he said gruffly.

She rubbed her cheek against his chest. "You smell like a man."

An abrupt shout of laughter escaped him. "Should I be offended?"

Her long, slender fingers unfastened one of his shirt buttons halfway down his chest and reached inside the fabric to play with his hair. He shivered, and his arms tightened until he heard her instinctive protest.

"Sorry." He eased his hold slightly.

She opened another button. "I like the way you smell. With some men it's like they've bathed in aftershave. You're very different."

He managed a rusty chuckle. "I'm not sure how to respond to that."

Her fingers continued their desultory exploration, and sweat broke out on his forehead.

She sighed. "When I get close to you it's like the scent of warm summer rain, or a spruce forest. I bet it's that pheromone thing. You know . . . my libido getting triggered by your raw animal scent. It makes me want to—"

She stopped abruptly, just when the conversation was getting interesting.

Her head was bent, and he pressed his lips to the gold and diamond clasp on her pearls. The nape of her neck looked infinitely fragile in the moonlight.

When his lips touched her skin, she moaned. At least he thought she did. She made some kind of sound, but smothered it quickly as though she was embarrassed. It was worth an experiment. He kissed her again . . . at the exact same spot.

This time the moan segued into a whimper. He had enough experience to peg this one. His little princess was aroused.

Before he could say or do anything, her head came up, nearly whacking his chin. Her lips were near his ear, and it was his turn to shiver.

She leaned closer. Her whisper tickled his earlobe. "Do you think you're ever going to kiss me?"

As his daddy would say, it was time to fish or cut bait. He leaned her back over his right arm. Now he could see her face clearly, the silvery light of the moon turning her skin as luminous as the pearls she wore.

A small, knowing smile curled her beautiful lips. Having his shy princess look at him with seduction in her eyes nearly sent him over the edge.

He cleared his throat. "I'm enjoying the moment." As a young boy he had always saved one of his Christmas presents to open just before bedtime on Christmas night. He'd savored the anticipation, though his siblings thought he was crazy. It made perfect sense to him.

Ever so slowly he bent his head. His chest was tight, and he was blind to his surroundings. His entire focus narrowed to Catherine's face. She slipped an arm around his neck and closed the distance between them. "Do it, for pete's sake," she groaned.

Their mouths met, separated, and then clung. There was a ringing in his ears, and he was shaking. He tried to hold back . . . remembering her fears, but apparently she had resolved whatever reservations she might have had.

His princess was killing him bit by bit, her hungry mouth tangling with his in urgent, passionate forays. She tasted sweet as honey and hot as fire. He slid his tongue deep in her mouth, and now he groaned as she tugged on it with her teeth.

He slid a hand beneath her sweater and touched her smooth, flat stomach. Her skin was warm silk beneath his fingers. When she didn't protest, his hand moved higher, thrusting aside the flimsy cup of her bra and taking a sweet handful of warm, soft woman.

When his thumb found her nipple, she arched her back and turned her head, burying her mouth against his arm. But she wasn't able to muffle the panting sounds that told him she was on the edge.

No longer thinking straight, he released her breast and slid a hand between her legs, cursing the fact that she wasn't wearing a dress. He pressed the seam of her pants, rubbing his hand against the thin fabric until she climaxed with a soft cry.

He held her tightly until the last of the tremors faded away. Then he stood and gently sat her on the bench before kneeling in front of her and burying his face in her lap.

Her arms came around his shoulders, and he felt her hands in his hair, massaging his head and scalp, stroking his neck. He was on such a hair trigger, it was almost enough to make him come.

He turned his face sideways so she could hear him. "Don't be afraid of this, Catherine," he begged.

Her hand cupped his cheek, and she traced the curve of

his lips with a fingertip. She was silent for a long time, and his stomach dropped in dismay. Had he come on too strong? But, no . . . his pretty princess had been a willing participant. Well, he amended honestly, at least until the end. He really hadn't given her much of a chance to protest that last part.

He lifted his head. "Catherine?"

She pushed him back down, continuing her steady massage. He felt her move restlessly, and his hands gripped her hips instinctively.

She played with his ears. He wondered why he never realized before that they were an erogenous zone. His cock was so hard, he felt like it might burst.

She slipped both hands into the neck of his shirt and used her fingers to work at the knots in his shoulders. When he yelped in pain, she laughed softly. "Don't be such a baby." More pressure. Now more of a caress.

Then she paused, and her hands slid up to cup his neck, her thumbs rubbing just at the base of his ears. She leaned down and kissed the top of his head. "I'm not afraid of this, Phillip. Not anymore."

"Good." He swallowed hard. "That's good."

She moved her hands to his chin. With two fingers, she separated his lips and probed in his mouth. He sucked greedily at her fingertips, biting gently. He lifted his head suddenly, dislodging her hands. He grasped her waist, lifted her sweater, and buried his mouth against her belly. He sucked at her flesh . . . hard enough to leave a mark. He felt starved, uncivilized.

She pulled his hair, whispering his name raggedly. He reached behind her and unfastened the clasp of her bra. Her modest flesh filled his hands. He tugged at the nipples and then tasted them.

Catherine cried out, and the tips of her breasts hardened. He grazed them with his teeth, taking her higher. She chanted his name in broken sobs.

He dragged her head down and kissed her wildly, using his tongue to mimic the act he wanted to complete.

She stood up and tugged at his arms, breaking the kiss momentarily. He joined her and pulled her into his embrace. Her smile poured gasoline on the fire. It was a sultry, self-satisfied gleam. His little princess was having fun torturing him.

He lifted her chin. "You're driving me crazy, Catherine."

Her eyes were dreamy. "Come inside with me."

He froze, standing at the edge of a chasm that threatened to pull him under. Four little words. Had any man living ever faced such temptation? The yearning threatened to tear him apart. Catherine's arms, Catherine's bed, Catherine's soft, welcoming body opening to his, taking him deep. He shook his head, instinctively backing away. "We can't."

She nipped his chin with her straight white teeth. "Why?"

"You'll regret it in the morning. I know you."

"Let's think about now."

The coaxing words of a temptress. How much could a man be expected to endure?

He shook his head blindly, trying to disengage himself

from her slender arms. He stepped backward, almost tripping over the fountain. For a moment he contemplated wading into it just to douse the flames consuming his body. He held up his hands, stopping her in her tracks.

And then her face changed. It was as if she snapped out of a trance. A succession of emotions chased across her face. Mortification. Embarrassment. Horror. And at the last . . . shame.

He couldn't allow that. "Dammit, Catherine. Don't you dare give me that look. I want to screw you till the sun comes up. I want it more than life itself. I am *not* rejecting you, honey."

Now confusion entered her gaze. At least that was an improvement over the devastated expression she'd worn a moment before.

He spoke slowly, not daring to touch her. "I want to make love to you, Catherine. I've wanted that for months. But we've waited this long . . . let's not rush it."

She frowned. "I know what I'm doing, Phillip. I'm neither a child nor a virgin. And I'm not drunk. Two glasses of wine aren't too much for me to handle."

He sighed. "I never said they were. But you seem like a woman who doesn't make rash decisions. I don't want to be something or someone you'll regret in the morning. Whatever this promise you made concerning me . . . let's not allow that to come into play here. This is between you and me. And this is important. Let's take our time. Let's savor what we're learning about each other. I don't even know your favorite color."

She cocked her head. "Yellow. Crunchy peanut butter. Vanilla. Original recipe. Chanel No. 5. The Dave Matthews Band. Nora Roberts. French Polynesia."

He shoved his hand in his pockets to keep them out of trouble. "What's the significance of that last one?"

She grinned, her arms crossed at her waist. "I'll tell you one day when we're better acquainted."

He rocked back on his heels. "That sounds promising. Will I like the answer?"

"I hope so." She took a step forward, and he backed away, cursing when she laughed at him.

He frowned fiercely. "Dammit, Catherine. I'm trying to be a gentleman. Or at least an honorable man."

She touched his Adam's apple with a fingertip, scraping lightly down to where his shirt was buttoned. "I have always been a circumspect, Goody Two-shoes. And where has it gotten me?"

He swallowed hard. "You're perfect in every way," he muttered. "I wouldn't change a thing."

She moved closer and kissed him very softly, her breasts barely brushing his chest. "Could I change your mind?"

"Yes." He ground out the words through clenched teeth. "But please don't."

She laid her head on his shoulder, and he had to touch her. He pulled his hands out of his pockets to hold her tight. There was no way she could miss his boner. He rubbed it against her belly and nearly caved. God, he wanted her.

She nuzzled her cheek against his chest like an affectionate cat. "Thank you for not giving up on me, Phillip Trent."

He chuckled. "Thank you for seeking me out, Catherine Maderis."

She spoke again, her voice dreamy. "It's going to be fabulous, isn't it?"

"What is?" he said, almost afraid to ask.

"When we make love for the first time."

His knees threatened to buckle. "Can we please talk about something else?"

"It's all I can think about."

He groaned and found her mouth blindly, kissing her and kissing her and kissing her, and then pushing her away and heading for his car as though all the hounds of hell were at his heels.

Three

The date of the museum's masked ball was a little more than two weeks after the incredible night that Phillip escaped from her garden.

For Catherine they were at once the most excruciating and most euphoric weeks of her life. She decided that Phillip was correct. Anticipation *was* a wonderful thing. She had cleared the first hurdle. Now she had to prepare for making her fantasy come true.

She had barely slept after he left her that evening. Her body was hot and achy, and in her mind she replayed his kisses a thousand times. She'd been right about the sexual chemistry between them. It was powerful. She'd never experienced anything like it. If Phillip had pressed the issue, she would have had sex with him right there in the garden.

It was a sobering thought, especially for a woman who was so shy she had hated undressing in front of other girls in gym class. She was inhibited and reserved by nature. Self-contained . . . not accustomed to throwing caution to the wind.

But when Phillip touched her, she turned into someone else entirely. She'd known it could happen. What she hadn't realized was how exhilarating a rush it would be. It had taken courage to contact Phillip. Being in his arms had taken none at all.

She got to work fifteen minutes late the morning after their date. That in itself was unusual. Apparently, pursuing a fantasy had all sorts of ramifications. As she checked e-mail, one jumped out at her. The subject line said, *About last night . . .*

Her heart began to pound, and she blushed, even though no one was around to see her. Phillip was a gentleman. He wouldn't put anything inappropriate in an e-mail. Would he?

She grinned at his screen name . . . PT109. Obviously Phillip Trent was a fan of JFK. She double-clicked, and his message appeared.

> Good morning, Princess. I'm sending you this e-mail from the plane. I'm off to Brussels and then London to meet with some foreign investors. The timing sucks, but this trip has been on the books for weeks, and I couldn't rearrange on such short notice. Believe me—I'd rather be there with you. I'd planned on telling you about it last night, but we got . . . distracted.
>
> Do you have a costume idea in mind for the

ball? I think you'd make a great princess. Why
don't you wear a pretty dress and I'll sup-
ply the props???

Don't count on me calling you. With my
schedule and the time change, it'll be imprac-
tical. But know that you are on my mind . . .
P.T.

She stared at the screen for long minutes with a goofy
smile on her face. Then she printed out the e-mail and put
it in her purse before deleting it. She would send him a
brief note later. When she figured out what to say.

The days flew past. Work kept her extremely busy,
which was a good thing. She had lunch with Kallie and
Gina twice. She didn't mention Phillip, and no one brought
up the pact. It would never have occurred to either of her
two friends that she had already begun fulfilling her end of
the deal.

Part of her wanted to tell them about Phillip, but another part wanted to hold the delicious secret close to her
heart. Talking about the fantasy might rob some of the
magic, and if things didn't go well, she'd just as soon not
have anyone know.

Phillip e-mailed her once a day. Most of them were
short and clearly written on the run. She answered him in
equally brief notes. It was difficult to frame sentences in
anything but impersonal terms.

About a week after his departure she found a package

waiting when she got home. It was a flat, shirt-style box. She ripped into the Tyvek covering and inside found elegant wrapping paper, cream striped with gold. She separated the taped edges carefully and finally lifted the lid. On top of pristine tissue was a tiny envelope. The small formal card inside was covered with heavy male handwriting.

I saw this and thought of you. The trim is antique Brussels lace. Don't forget me . . . P.T.

She folded back the tissue and lifted out a garment so delicate it felt like nothing in her hands. It was a white lawn nightgown in the style of a poet's shirt, the fabric so fine it was almost transparent. She held it up to her shoulders . . . it fell just below the knee. The sweet fragrance of lavender teased her nose, and she realized the lovely, sheer cloth had picked up the scent of the expensive tissue.

Phillip Trent was full of surprises. Most men might have picked out a sexy, skimpy negligee. Phillip's choice was feminine and beautiful and quite perfect. It showed that he knew far more about her than she realized.

She clutched the cobweb-soft garment to her breast and shivered. She was building a fantasy in her head that reality might have a hard time living up to. Phillip Trent was a flesh-and-blood man. He had flaws and shortcomings like everyone else.

But he made her feel so alive, so naughty, so completely female.

On day ten, her phone rang at three a.m. She fumbled

for the receiver with her heart racing, hoping it wasn't an emergency.

"Hello."

The voice on the other end was clear and strong. "Catherine . . . it's Phillip."

She sat up, shoving her hair back from her face. "Phillip. How are you?" He sounded stressed.

"I'm sorry to wake you."

"It's okay."

"I wanted to hear your voice."

Her nipples tightened. "I'm glad you called," she said softly.

He muttered something muffled. "I feel like I've been gone a month." A long silence followed, and then he said, "Have you missed me?"

His question made her catch her breath, but she opted for honesty. "Every second of every day."

He groaned. "God, sweetheart. All I can think about is what an idiot I was to leave you that night."

She smiled, even though he couldn't see it. "I hate to say it, but I think you were right. We barely even know each other."

"Not true. I've been studying you for months."

Her smile grew bigger. "That's not quite the same as spending time together."

"I think we just skipped over a few of the social conventions. Why waste time with inconsequential stuff? I rather enjoyed our *get-acquainted* time."

"You're a naughty man."

His laugh was a low rumble. "I could be even naughtier given half a chance."

"That sounds promising."

There was a noise in the background, and he mumbled something under his breath. "I've got to go, honey. I'll be home day after tomorrow. Let's have dinner together."

Her heart skipped a beat. "The dance is only a few days away. Let's hold off until then."

He groaned. "You're killing me, Catherine. I can't wait to hold you in my arms again."

"Aren't you the one who gave me the speech about anticipation?" she teased.

"I must have been out of my mind."

She chuckled. "Would it help if I tell you I'm wearing your gift?"

His end of the line went silent, and she wondered if they had been disconnected.

"Phillip?"

She heard him clear his throat. "You liked it, then?" He sounded surprisingly diffident.

"I loved it. It's the most beautiful thing I've ever owned. You did good, Mr. Trent." She tried lightening the mood.

"I can't decide what I want more . . . to see you in it or out of it."

"Why, Mr. Trent. How forward of you. I didn't know your present came with strings attached. I've heard about men like you."

"And what did you hear?"

"That they're good in bed."

This time the silence was longer.

When he finally responded, the heat in his voice threatened to melt the phone wires. "With you, Princess, I can guarantee it."

The afternoon of the ball, Catherine forced herself to eat a light meal. There would be a buffet later, but she didn't want to waste time eating when she could be dancing with Phillip. And besides, her stomach was doing such crazy flip-flops, food wasn't all that appealing.

She washed and dried her hair and, instead of letting it curve as usual at her shoulders, pulled it on top of her head and let a few tendrils curl at her ears and neck. She put on the strand of pearls her parents had given her for her twenty-first birthday and added a small pair of old-fashioned pearl and diamond earrings she had inherited from her great-aunt.

Her dress was a fairy tale. Phillip had suggested the princess idea, and she had complied. The gown was strapless ice blue satin. The full skirt billowed into a romantic cloud underlaid with layers of tulle petticoats. She left her hands and arms bare of jewelry and donned a pair of elbow-length gloves that had been dyed to match the dress.

She wanted to be comfortable, so instead of pumps or sandals, she wore low-heeled ballet slippers in the same shade of blue. The pièce de résistance for her fantasy evening was a cream satin eye mask edged in tiny faux pearls.

It wasn't important that she wear it now, or even when Phillip saw her for the first time. But later . . . when the formal part of the evening was over, the mask would be essential.

He called her at half past six to make sure things were on schedule. They'd had no contact since his transatlantic phone call. She left the street door unlocked and told him to let himself in.

Phillip ran a finger around the collar of his tux shirt and tugged at his bow tie. He was no stranger to formal dress, but tonight the damned thing was choking him. He'd finished up at the gym two hours ago after a grueling session of kickboxing, weight lifting, and laps in the pool.

He was so hyped up he felt as if he had consumed a year's worth of caffeine and sugar. The hard labor at the gym was supposed to mellow him out, but if it had worked at all, he couldn't tell. He'd grabbed a veggie burger at the gym deli and gone home to shower and shave.

Now he was in his car headed over to Catherine's. He had damp palms and a shaky pulse. All he needed was a case of acne, and it would have been high school all over again. He was so nervous, it was a miracle he managed to stop at every light.

His business associates would be shocked to see him now. Phillip Trent had a reputation for being ice cold under pressure. He'd practically invented the "never let them see you sweat" mantra.

But business was business, and this was Catherine. Catherine, the cool beautiful object of all his fantasies. Catherine, the shy, yet plucky woman who seemed determined to push all his buttons. Catherine, the princess waiting in her tower for him to climb the wall.

He parked and entered the garden, locking the door behind him. He walked up the front steps and took a deep breath before knocking twice to announce his presence. In the foyer, he stood hesitantly trying to decide if he should cool his heels in the drawing room or find her in her bedroom. Before he could come to a decision, a sound at the top of the stairs drew his attention.

His gaze snapped upward where Catherine stood poised on the top step. She looked regal, elegant. He felt like a peasant waiting for an audience with the queen.

He ran a finger around his collar again. "Hello, Catherine."

"Hi." Her voice sounded breathless, and he wondered if she was a fraction as excited as he was.

She descended the steps slowly, never breaking eye contact. She was graceful and sure, her steps unfaltering. When she was on eye level with him, two steps from the bottom, she stopped.

He laid a hand on the newel post at the foot of the banister. "You look amazing."

A spot of color bloomed on each of her cheeks. "Thank you, Phillip. I know men hate dressing up, but seeing you in that tux almost makes me swoon."

He grinned. "Almost?"

She raised an eyebrow. "We twenty-first-century women aren't such fragile flowers as our predecessors."

He stepped closer, noticing the tiny pulse at her throat . . . the pearls. The gentle curve of her breasts. Her narrow waist. And those gloves . . .

He swallowed and reached in his jacket pocket for a small muslin bag. He handed it to Catherine. "I promised to bring the props."

She opened the drawstring and pulled out a simple tiara. It was made of delicate tear-shaped diamonds and accented with pearls.

"Phillip." Catherine's cry of pleasure made him smile. She touched the stones reverently. "It's exquisite. Where on earth did you get this?"

"It belonged to my grandmother. She liked to brag about how she had a distant connection to some branch of French royalty. So one Christmas, as a joke, my grandpa gave her this tiara."

"Some joke."

He stepped closer. "Let me help you put it on. We don't want to mess up your hair." He set it on her head and gently pressed down until the tortoiseshell combs on either side were hidden.

She tilted her nose and lifted her chin. "Well?"

He tapped her cheek. "Perfect."

Taking him off guard, she caught his face between her hands. "Don't I get a hello kiss?"

Their gazes clashed, banked hunger in his, feminine pique in hers. "I don't want to ruin your makeup."

"I haven't even put on my lipstick," she pointed out.

He hadn't noticed. Her mouth was all soft, rosy temptation.

She didn't close her eyes. Instead, she dragged him closer bit by bit, perhaps waiting for him to renew his protest.

He wasn't stupid.

Their lips met, and they groaned in unison. He slanted his head and wrapped his arms around her waist, lifting her on tiptoe. The damned skirt was so big it practically swallowed his legs. Perhaps the princess thing had a few drawbacks.

And then he forgot to think at all when Catherine's tongue slipped between his lips and teased the inside of his mouth. His brain went fuzzy, and all the workouts in the world weren't enough to make his cock too tired to spring to attention.

He was starved for her. A week and a half in Europe had seemed like the worst kind of exile. He released her lips and buried his face in her shoulder. How could skin be so soft? He dragged his mouth from her collarbone to earlobe, nibbling as he went.

Her hands were in his hair, doing that massage thing that drove him crazy. He scooped her into his arms and carried her to the drawing room. The biggest piece of furniture in the room was an uncomfortable Victorian sofa. He perched there, cradling her against his chest.

She glanced at the clock on the mantel and sighed. "I hate to be the voice of reason, but we can't be late. My boss expects to see me there for the mix and mingle at the beginning."

His arms tightened for one last second, and then he helped her to her feet with a disgruntled frown. "How long do we have to stay?"

She leaned against him. "Two or three hours. It won't be so bad."

He took her hand and pressed it against his fly. "Easy for you to say."

Her shocked gasp made him ashamed of his crass behavior, but she dropped to her knees in a cloud of blue. "Poor fellow." She touched her lips to the cloth of his trousers, right at the fly. His knees locked, and his eyes threatened to roll back in his head.

He pulled her to her feet none too gently. "That's not helping," he bit out.

She went up on her tiptoes again. "Another kiss?"

He backed away. "No, dammit. Go paint your lips and let's get out of here."

The last thing he heard as she disappeared upstairs was the tinkle of her laughter.

The ball was being held at one of the fine old Charleston mansions, long since transformed into a museum. The chandeliers sparkled. A string quartet filled the air with music, and the female guests were a swarm of rainbow butterflies against the sober black of their escorts. Very few of the

sophisticated patrons had elected to wear elaborate cos-
tumes. Most had decided to settle for simple masks.

Catherine was the most beautiful woman there, hands
down. He had admired her before, but watching her now,
seeing how she drew people together, introduced who needed
to meet whom, made light conversation with important
donors . . . well, he was impressed. In light of what she had
told him about her shyness growing up, he had to respect
the effort it took for her to do her job, when clearly she
would prefer a less prominent role.

But the strain of being in party mode when that wasn't
her personality began to take its toll after a couple of hours.
He could see it in her face.

He snagged her arm and drew her toward the anteroom
where the food was laid out. "You need to eat something,
honey." She allowed him to fill a plate for her. When he
glanced sideways, her eyes were closed, and she was rolling
her neck from side to side.

He balanced two plates and one glass of champagne.
Catherine carried the other flute and followed him docilely
through a set of French doors onto the patio where tables
were scattered about. He found a tiny one big enough only
for two. He wanted her to himself.

When they were seated, she took a drink of bubbly and
sighed long and deep.

He examined her slight pallor. "This is very difficult for
you, isn't it?"

She opened her mouth to protest, but he shushed her
with a finger on her lips. "Don't lie to me. You were fantastic

in there. Your boss should give you a damned raise, but you hated it."

Her eyes darkened, and she dropped her head.

He caressed her cheek. "It wasn't a criticism, sweetheart. You did your job, and you did it beautifully, but I could tell you weren't having fun."

She shrugged slightly. "Work isn't always fun. Events like this only take place a couple of nights a year. The rest of the time they leave me alone in peace to tend to my books and papers and artifacts."

Suddenly he realized something he hadn't fully understood before. "It took a lot of courage for you to come to my office, didn't it?"

Her lips twisted ruefully. "Yes."

"And Belinda turned you away."

She must have seen the regret in his eyes, because she smiled. "Don't sweat it, Mr. Trent. You were worth it."

He chuckled. "That remains to be seen."

He loved making her blush. She took a bite of her beef brochette and ignored him pointedly.

They ate in silence for several minutes. The music was fainter out here, the air sweeter and fresher. Overhead, visible between the branches that sported spring green, a handful of stars twinkled.

He glanced at his watch. "The dancing should be getting ready to start. Shall we?"

She dabbed her lips daintily. "Of course."

She reached in his pocket to retrieve the two masks

she had tucked there earlier. His was plain black, hers ivory with pearls. A number of the guests had worn masks all evening, but since Catherine was actually on the clock, she had preferred to save hers for the evening's entertainment.

He helped her slip it on and then donned his. His gut tightened when he looked at her. How could a small eye mask make her look even more dangerously sexy? She could have been a French spy in the midst of the Revolution. He lifted her gloved hand to his lips.

"Would mademoiselle like to dance?"

She nodded her head regally. "Oui."

He took her arm in his and led her back inside.

The moment Catherine donned her mask, she relaxed. For some bizarre reason, it freed her, made her feel reckless. Which was a wonderful thing, because for the fantasy to succeed, the shy, uptight Catherine needed to be locked in a closet. Her daring counterpart would hold center stage for the remainder of the evening.

She had expected Phillip to be a divine dancer. In truth, he was a bit awkward, and that endearing masculine vulnerability made her like him even more.

They circled among their fellow dancers as one waltz led to another. The ball's planning committee members were made up of the Charleston old guard, and the music never strayed from show tunes, famous movie scores, and the romantic classics.

Phillip steered her with confidence around the room, and she knew in her heart that she would always feel safe in his arms. He was a protector by nature. He treated her as an equal, but she knew he wouldn't hesitate to step in if anything threatened her.

One of his big hands rested at her waist and the other roved back and forth over her bare back. Every touch sent her temperature higher. Her voluminous dress felt too hot, the pins in her hair too confining.

But she restrained her impatience with the knowledge that her fantasy evening would have one and only one possible conclusion.

They paused occasionally to sip a drink or chat with an acquaintance. And then they danced some more. Being held by Phillip Trent as the evening drifted away was a kind of fantasy in itself. He made her laugh. He made her yearn. And when he stole a kiss from time to time in a shadowed corner of the room, he made her burn.

At eleven she decided she had done her duty. Phillip had been waylaid for the moment by a business associate and was doing a commendable job of persuading the man to increase the size of his donation to the museum.

She excused herself to visit the ladies' room. In the mirror, the lady with the mask seemed like a glamorous stranger. Her lips curved in a sensuous smile, and her eyes glittered with excitement. She didn't look a bit like someone who would be content to hide in a corner.

When she found Phillip again, he was laughing out loud, his head thrown back, his teeth gleaming. She stopped in her tracks and put a hand to her heart, feeling suddenly breathless. How could such an incredible physical specimen, such a strikingly handsome, virile man be interested in her?

She stomped on the old feelings of inadequacy and lifted her chin, sailing across the room to stand by his side. He slid an arm around her waist with casual ease, listening as the other man finished his anecdote. She leaned her head against his shoulder and smiled.

Moments later Phillip made their excuses and steered her toward the exit. On the porch of the antebellum home, they paused, and he leaned back against a column, pulling her between his legs.

He touched her face. "Ready to take the mask off, sweetheart?"

"No. It stays on."

He frowned. "Why?"

She smiled recklessly. "Because the Catherine in the mask plans to do a lot of things this evening that the shy Catherine might not have the courage to do."

His eyes went black with shock. She saw muscles work in his throat. "And my mask?"

She shrugged. "Your call."

He ripped it off and shoved it in his pocket, rumpling his hair in the process. His eyes focused on her mouth, yearning written in every plane of his face. "I'm almost afraid to touch you, Princess. You look too beautiful for words."

"I think you might change your mind," she said huskily.

He lifted an eyebrow in silent inquiry.

She slid her arms beneath his jacket and cuddled him close. "I'm not wearing a stitch beneath this dress."

Four

Phillip felt his body tighten from head to toe. He wasn't sure he had heard her correctly. "You're—"

"Nude. Bare as a baby's bottom. Au naturel. In my birthday suit. Shall I go on?"

He choked out a laugh, sliding his hands down over her hips. "I get the picture." He bunched the cloth of her skirt in his fists. "How am I supposed to know you're telling the truth? This thing has more layers than a prize-winning onion."

She kissed his chin. "There are other ways to find out."

"That might involve you removing the dress," he said, holding his breath for her answer.

This time her sharp little teeth nipped his chin. "I'm counting on it."

Okay, Phillip. Don't lose your cool. He released her skirt and placed a hand on either side of her neck, bending down to kiss her. He was so hard, it was difficult to stand up straight. And for some reason the evening seemed to be escaping his control.

He couldn't think beyond this moment, couldn't visual-ize how he was going to get her somewhere they could be alone.

The kiss made things worse. He'd had only one glass of champagne, but his thinking was foggy. He drew back and played with one of her earrings, trying to catch his breath. "Where were you thinking of taking this party . . . back to your house?" He remembered the mosquito-netted bed and thought he might have the willpower to make it that far be-fore he stripped her.

She shook her head. "I was hoping we could go to your boat."

He stroked the line where the bodice of her dress ended and smooth, creamy skin began. "I'm not prepared for a nighttime trip."

She touched his straining erection. "I wasn't planning on going anywhere. If your hands were on the wheel, you'd be too busy for what I have in mind."

He cleared his throat. "Oh, well . . ."

"Phillip." She looked up at him. Her eyes through the slits in her mask were deep pools of mystery in the semi-darkness. "Do you have the car keys?"

"Hmm? What? Oh . . . yeah . . ." He was having trouble breathing, so he removed his bow tie.

Catherine giggled and steered him down the steps to the street. The short walk to the car did nothing to clear his head.

He stopped before opening the car door and jerked her

into his arms, kissing her hard. She didn't protest. Her sweet lips opened for his invasion, and she met his passion with her own. He cupped her breasts through satin and squeezed.

She moaned but slid from his embrace, leaning against the hood of the car and breathing heavily. "The boat."

He nodded jerkily. After seating her and tucking in the yards of fabric that comprised her skirt, he got in and started the engine, grinding the gears before making it out of the parking space.

Catherine giggled again, but he was past caring.

At the marina, he parked and led her to the slip where the *Camelot* was berthed. He hopped across the rail, extended the walkway, and helped her board.

The harbor was quiet. Nearby boats bobbed gently in the late-night breeze. While he unlocked the cabin and turned on lights, Catherine wandered to the bow of the boat and rested her hands on the rail, looking out across the water. Far in the distance, a light from Fort Sumter marked its location.

From his vantage point, she looked almost like a lovely ghost, her skin and dress silvery pale in the ambient light from the nearby docks.

He joined her at the railing, resting his hands on her shoulders. He bent to kiss her cheek. "I promise I'll take you on a night cruise one evening."

She turned to face him. "Can we anchor somewhere and swim in the ocean?"

He nodded slowly, imagining the feel of her slick wet body in his arms. "Sure," he said gruffly.

She looked at the boats on either side of them. "No one seems to be around tonight."

"Maybe earlier. Not at this hour."

She laid a gloved hand on his chest. "I have an idea, Phillip. Given the lack of spectators and the size of my skirt, it might be safe for you to check out my earlier claim, don't you think?"

Where her gloved hand touched him, his chest burned. The masked Catherine wasn't as familiar to him as her conservative twin. He gulped in a mouthful of air. "You mean . . ."

Her smile was pure seduction. "Lift my skirt. Touch me."

She turned her back to him and resumed her position at the rail. He glanced uneasily from side to side. They appeared to be entirely alone. Was his shy Catherine really so bold?

Was he prepared to indulge her risky request? Damned straight.

He rubbed her shoulders and ran his hands down to her wrists, leaning forward to whisper in her ear, "You're not to move, do you understand?"

She nodded slowly.

He tapped the back of her hands. "Whatever you do, don't let go of the railing." He saw her fingers clench involuntarily.

If he stood close to her back and gathered the fabric bit by bit, he could preserve the illusion of modesty and yet still give his hands free rein to explore.

Gradually, he lifted the heavy satin and crumpled the petticoats in his hands. The very bottom layer was a thin cotton designed to keep the scratchy, stiff netting from irritating her skin.

He lifted and bunched until he had the cotton lining in his palms. He stepped closer. Reaching down, he let the piles of fabric rest on his forearms as he gripped her bare ass.

She sucked in a breath. The sound echoed on the night air, and he hissed in her ear. "Quiet, Princess. Your life depends on it."

He initiated the game, and she followed his lead. She shuddered but remained mute as he had ordered. Gently he rubbed her soft bottom, squeezing and kneading the firm flesh. His thumbs eased down her crack, tracing the curve until it joined her thighs on either side.

Dropping to his knees, he licked and bit gently at each of her sweet rounded cheeks. Her legs were trembling. He balanced the fabric on his shoulders and went lower, his hands exploring first one calf and then the other, learning the shape and length of her legs.

He removed her slippers and massaged the arches of her feet. Gently, but firmly, he scooted her legs until she stood with her feet ten inches or so apart.

He paused for a moment and got to his feet, letting the skirt tumble to the deck. He bracketed her body with his, placing his hands over hers where they clutched the railing.

He pressed against her, wondering if she could feel his

cock through her dress. Doubtful, unless she was like that famous fairy-tale princess with the pea.

He kissed the side of her neck and bit her earlobe. "You dress like royalty on the outside, Princess, but beneath your fine clothes you have the body of a whore. Why else would you leave yourself open to the possibility of an easy tumble?"

His hands cradled her breasts, feeling her stiff nipples though the slick fabric.

Her head fell back against his shoulder. "I wanted to be ready for you, my prince."

He tugged at a nipple and pinched roughly. "I'm no prince. Quit trying to make me something I'm not. A humble gardener at your service, my liege."

She moaned as he played with her breasts. "Nothing humble about you," she panted. "The scullery maids talk of your size and prowess."

He wanted to feel her bare tits, but he dared not. Not in such an exposed place. He turned his words into a sneer. "And Your Highness wanted a roll in the hay? Is that it? Simple curiosity?"

She pressed her hips back against his, almost derailing his ability to converse. She spoke softly, but he could hear each word. "I wanted to be yours . . . in every way."

The simple statement affected him profoundly. Was his playacting princess speaking the truth? He dropped to his knees again and shoved the skirt away with rough haste. This time, he anchored one hand against her hip and let the other press between her thighs.

He groaned aloud. She was warm and silky smooth and wet with her own arousal. He slipped one finger between the soft folds of her femininity. She whimpered.

He added a finger and probed farther. His penis swelled and throbbed, desperate to be in on the action. Still deep inside her, he used his other hand to pet and stroke her, carefully avoiding her clitoris. He was working blind, the damn dress nearly smothering him.

Her knees almost buckled at one point, and he barked out a command. "Do . . . not . . . move."

"I can't bear it, gardener," she cried softly.

He parted her most intimate lips once again and renewed his assault. "You have no choice, little slut. Unless you wish for all the court to hear of your activities. You'll bow to my will, or I shall expose you as the tart you are."

He set up a rhythm with his fingers. Her inner flesh was swollen, so hot against his intrusion. Finally, when even he could bear it no longer, he touched her most sensitive nerves, pressing gently, stroking, scraping with his fingernail, until at last she gave a great shudder and climaxed with a muffled shriek.

She collapsed in his arms, drowning him in satin and tulle. He shook free and turned her, cradling her carefully as he sprawled backward against the wall of the cabin. Her chest heaved with panting breaths.

He brushed strands of hair from her forehead and rubbed her arms. The night air had turned cool, but her skin was damp and warm.

He touched her face. "May I remove the mask now?"

Her hand came up in protest. "No. I want to keep it for now. Please."

He frowned slightly. Surely she couldn't still be shy with him.

Reclining as they were, they had a tiny bit more privacy, but not much. He couldn't wait another second. He slid a hand beneath her, partially unzipping her dress. Then he edged the fabric downward until her breasts were free. Gently, reverently, he touched them one at a time. His throat closed up, and his mouth dried.

She was as beautiful as the sea at dawn, cream and rose and dusky shadows. He toyed with one raspberry nipple. "My princess is beautiful. It hurts to look at you."

She tugged his hand up to her lips and kissed it, drawing one of his fingers deep into her mouth. "Then you should do more touching and less looking," she mumbled.

Her words were slurred. He teased the tips of her breasts more roughly, testing their hardness against his palms. He slid one hand beneath her dress again, zeroing in on the spot he had pleasured before.

She moved restlessly. "I can't. Not so soon."

The note of petulance in her voice amused him. He touched her deliberately, wetting his finger with her juices and then stroking gently. "Have you forgotten so soon? Your wishes do not matter now . . . whatever I ask of you, you will do."

"But I—"

He lifted her shoulders and captured her mouth wildly,

one hand still trapped between her legs. "No arguments, woman," he ground out between kisses.

He traced her teeth with his tongue and then plunged it deep in her mouth as his hand did the same. Catherine's back bowed, and she writhed against him. He bit her earlobe and whispered, "Shatter, my blossom . . . I will gather the pieces and begin all over again."

This time he silenced her cries with his mouth. He was so hungry for her, he didn't know where one kiss stopped and another began. He staggered to his feet, stumbling and almost dropping her.

It shocked him into a moment of clarity. He gazed down at her face. "Shall I take you inside, Catherine?"

Her lips were swollen. Her tongue peeped out to wet them. "That would be a most desirable plan."

As Phillip carried her into the cabin and locked the door, she tried to gather her composure. Her dress was down around her waist, her breasts were swollen and tight, and despite two really amazing orgasms, her core ached with the need to have Phillip deep inside her.

She slumped on a banquette as she watched him draw the shades. The cabin was small but cozy. One wall boasted kitchen facilities. The other was made up of cabinets built around a small bed. The pilot house was above them, and narrow steps led down to the facilities.

Phillip paused in front of her, looking down at her with no discernible expression on his face. "No one can see us now."

God help her, those six quiet words sent her temperature flaming out of control once again. She sat up, clutching her bodice to her nude breasts in a pathetic show of modesty. "I think I'd like to visit the restroom."

He chuckled, his eyes cataloging her every move. "It's very small. You'll have to lose the dress."

"A robe?" she asked hopefully.

"Nope."

"Your jacket?"

"Maybe later . . . if you follow orders."

He pulled out a small wooden chair and seated himself, looking comfortable and relaxed. At least if one overlooked his white-knuckled fists and glittering eyes.

He waved a hand. "Undress for me, Princess."

She stood slowly, her stomach in a knot. One hand held up her dress, the other touched her mask for reassurance. What was there to take off? She was woefully unprepared for a strip show. She let her gown fall to the floor. The billowing satin came up to her knees, even then. She had to step out of it and kick it away. The tile beneath her bare feet was cold.

Phillip's jaw had hardened to granite. The front of his dress slacks tented in an alarming fashion. Her hands fluttered to cover her nakedness . . . at least down there. Phillip had already seen her breasts.

He cleared his throat and moved in his chair. "I'll wait while you freshen up."

It was agony to turn her back on him and walk away. She descended the four steps and tugged open the door of a tiny bathroom. The light came on automatically. She relieved herself and found a clean towel to wash up. She was happy to see there was no mirror. She didn't want to know what she looked like.

When she could postpone it no longer, she returned to the cabin. Phillip hadn't moved. His stare was laser sharp, his cheekbones streaked with color.

She had expected him to ask her to take down her hair as part of a common male fantasy. But Phillip had other plans.

He looked her over from head to toe and smiled. It was not the smile of a gentleman. He pointed to the floor. "Put the dress back on."

Puzzled, she did as he demanded, crossing to his chair and presenting her back so he could zip her up. When she was clothed once again, he squeezed her elbow. "Take off my jacket."

She relaxed a fraction as she stepped behind him and complied. She folded the coat carefully and laid it on the counter.

He was still facing away from her. "Now my tie and shirt."

She slid her arms around his neck, unfastened his tie, and loosened the studs from his shirt, then put them with his coat.

He stood up suddenly, startling her. With one practiced move, he shrugged out of his shirt and discarded his cummerbund. His broad chest was muscular and lightly dusted with dark hair. She watched, mesmerized, as his hands went to his fly. He unfastened the button at his waist.

But then he stopped. "I believe the princess can do this next part."

She approached him slowly and didn't protest when his hands touched her shoulders and pushed her to her knees. She lowered his zipper, holding her breath as his black briefs appeared, stretched to capacity by a fully erect, impressively large penis.

She hesitated, and he circled the shell of her ear with his fingertip. "That's enough."

"But you're—"

His fists clenched at his sides. "I said enough, Princess."

He helped her to her feet.

She looked up at him helplessly, snared in a trap of her own making. She wanted him to do something, anything. This slow crescendo was driving her insane.

He pulled her close. Her cheek rested against the hard planes of his chest. She inhaled his familiar scent. Everything about him was hard and strong.

He tipped up her chin. "Close your eyes, Princess."

She obeyed reluctantly. She heard him move away and then return seconds later.

He touched her eyelashes. "Look at me," he said hoarsely. He had donned his mask, and with his bare chest, he looked like a pirate intent on plunder. Her stomach gave a little flip, and she shivered.

His frown was black. "No fear, Catherine. Not now. "Only pleasure."

He kissed her, and his mask tickled her face. Partially undressed, he no longer seemed like the Phillip Trent she knew. His mouth drugged her, every caress of his lips deeper and more carnal than the last. She whimpered, trying desperately to get closer.

He held her at arm's length suddenly, his chest heaving. "Kneel by the bed, my princess."

She moved instinctively, never dreaming of outright disobedience. She fell to her knees and fussed with her skirts until they surrounded her without hampering her movement.

He moved behind her. "Lean forward."

The bed was a bit higher than normal because of the drawers beneath it. It supported her comfortably as she bent at the waist.

She felt his hands lift her skirts and tumble them across her back.

He murmured something and then she felt two large, warm hands on her thighs. "Spread them."

She moved awkwardly. Not being able to see him or what he was doing was incredibly erotic. Her breath was coming rapidly.

He tapped the insides of her knees, and she gave him two more inches. She felt him position himself against the back of her legs, the hair on his thighs tickling hers. The weight of his erection rested against the crease of her bottom.

He leaned forward, his breath hot in her ear. "I want to screw you like this, my princess, wearing your tiara. So that when I'm dripping with sweat, toiling in the hot dirt of your summer garden, I can remember the screams of the whore who thinks she's a princess."

Without warning, he separated her folds and plunged

deep, all the way to the hilt. The intrusion was shocking, rough, and, god help her, painfully arousing. She felt him shaking, and she knew without asking that he was on the edge.

"How dare you, gardener?" she hissed. "How dare you treat me so crudely?"

His cock flexed, and he surged deeper. "Your pretty diamonds and pearls mean nothing to me," he panted. "You're an easy lay the same as all of them."

She squeezed hard with her inner muscles and heard him draw in a shallow breath. "I wouldn't be so sure."

She took him by surprise, rolling from his embrace and jumping to her feet. She backed toward the door, reaching behind her for the knob. "I don't want you anymore," she pouted. "You're common and coarse."

He had stumbled backward onto his butt, but now he stood, his hands at his hips, his unfastened trousers framing a hungry cock. "Come here, my pretty princess," he growled.

She stamped her foot. "No. Never."

He moved closer, stalking her. "Never is a long time."

She held out a hand. "Stay where you are. I command you." He chuckled, and the hair on her arms stood up.

He reached down and stroked himself. "I'm in pain, Princess. You're responsible. It's time to pay the price for your teasing and taunts."

She lifted her chin. "I'll scream."

"And I'll point out that your fine undergarments are still in your room back at the castle. Naughty princess. What will everyone think?"

She had run out of options. She lifted her chin. "Very well. Get it over with."

She closed her eyes and did her best to project haughty boredom.

When his hands touched her, she yelped.

He laughed and captured her mouth. "Kiss me, little shrew."

He moved his hips against her, and she wanted to rip the dress from her body. "I can't feel you," she moaned. "Unzip me."

He nibbled her ear. "No time," he muttered. "I want you now."

One last time he found his way beneath her skirts and lifted her legs around his waist. He positioned the head of his cock at her entrance and went still.

She beat at his shoulders in a frenzy of frustration. "Now, Phillip. Now."

His chuckle was rusty, his chest heaving with labored breaths. This time there was no quick entry. This time he eased forward with torturous slowness, claiming her in breath-stealing increments.

When he had joined their bodies completely, her head fell forward, resting on his collarbone. "More," she demanded shakily, hearing the exhaustion in her own voice. "More."

At last he released the tight control he held over his body and pounded into her, pressing her back against the door, his fingers digging into the backs of her quivering thighs.

Sweat dampened the hair at his temples. "Come for me, Princess," he begged hoarsely, his voice almost unrecognizable.

Again and again he thrust. Heat spiraled from deep in her womb to every cell in her body. Incredible pleasure built and swelled, tearing her apart, frightening her with its intensity.

And then her vision went dark and the stars cart-wheeled inside her head as she fell off the edge of a pinnacle and floated back to earth.

When Phillip could breathe again, he slipped from her body and scooped her into his arms. He laid her on the bed and fetched a damp towel to clean them both.

Her eyes were closed, and she had turned on her side, her cheek resting on one hand like a child.

He left her dress in place, not wanting to wake her. Gently, he removed the tiara and, finally, the mask. "We don't need this anymore," he whispered, smoothing her hair.

And then he climbed in beside her, pulled up the covers, and held her close as he slid into a deep, satiated sleep.

Five

Phillip yawned and stretched, disoriented for a moment by the gentle sway of his bed. He blinked, and memory returned. Catherine . . .

He reached for her and found nothing but cold, empty sheets. Frowning, he sat up and examined his surroundings. His own clothes were scattered. Catherine's dress was nowhere to be seen. If she had gone to the head, she had taken her dress with her.

He wasn't alarmed at first. She struck him as the kind of woman who would enjoy the early morning. Perhaps she had merely gone outside.

He used the facilities, splashed water on his face, and got dressed in last night's clothing . . . everything but his jacket and tie. When he could postpone it no longer, he stepped out onto the deck. He had a nasty feeling in the pit of his stomach, and he was in no hurry to confirm his suspicions.

It didn't take long to search the boat. Catherine wasn't enjoying the crisp morning.

Near the bow, half caught beneath a coil of rope, he found one of her ballet slippers. In the dark, it would have been almost invisible. The thought of Catherine stealing away like a thief in the night, with one bare foot and no wrap, made his gut wrench.

Had she no thought at all for her personal safety? He stared down at the small shoe in his hand, stunned and sick at heart.

What had he done to make her run? Confused guilt fuzzed his logic and made nausea roll in his stomach. He'd considered last evening to be one of the best nights of his life. But perhaps the humble gardener and the untouchable princess was nothing more than a fantasy.

Anger shoved aside the hurt and disillusionment. Pretty Catherine owed him some answers.

He drove home on autopilot, absently making note of traffic lights and stop signs. It was Saturday morning, and traffic was light.

At his house, he stripped and stepped into a scalding shower, trying to thaw his numb emotions. Afterward he shaved and dressed in khakis and a thin cotton sweater. Socks and shoes. Keys. Cell phone.

He was back in the car in forty-five minutes. Breakfast didn't make the list. The thought of food was repugnant. A headache throbbed in his temples, and bands of tension crushed his skull.

He found a parking space at the curb near her door. He sat in the car for a long time, drumming his fingers on the steering wheel. He needed a plan. He was good at plans. Create a vision. Plan and execute. It was what he did.

But his brain was going in circles. He couldn't focus. He kept seeing her as she descended the steps in her house. Regal. Lovely. Sophisticated. Way out of his reach.

He dropped back his head and groaned. What would he say to her? Maybe he could just fling himself at her feet like a helpless supplicant. It had a certain dramatic flair he appreciated, but he was damned if he would crawl at this point.

He hadn't done anything wrong . . . or had he? Had he been too rough with her? Had he shocked her? He'd taken her from behind without even removing their clothes. She was a quiet, reserved woman . . . refined, a lady in the best sense of the word.

And he'd fucked her like a wild man. Oh, god . . .

When his own cowardice disgusted him beyond belief, he got out of the car and stared at his first hurdle. He could call her . . . ask her to unlock the gate and let him in, but he was afraid she might turn him away. And if he rang the bell, she might ignore it.

Glancing around to make sure he had no witnesses, he took out a credit card and jimmied the lock. It opened with alarming ease, and he vowed to make sure she installed something better ASAP.

He slipped inside and spotted her immediately. She was in a far corner of the garden watering her camellia bushes. No grubby jeans and sneakers for his pretty princess. She was dressed in cream linen slacks and a sleeveless coral linen top. Her hair was pulled back in a ponytail low on her neck. On her feet she wore canvas espadrilles. And of course, the familiar necklace.

She didn't hear him approach at first. When she did, she whirled around and her hands went to her throat, touching her pearls. The long-necked tin watering can fell unnoticed at her feet.

Something flashed in her eyes for a split second and her chin quivered, but before he could identify the emotions or even know for sure they were there, a pleasant mask descended over her features.

She even smiled. "Phillip. Good morning. You're out bright and early."

He stopped in his tracks, perplexed. Something wasn't right. He narrowed his eyes. "Catherine."

She waved a hand. "Can you believe how warm it is? The Weather Channel is saying we may set a record today. I think my crepe myrtles are going to bloom early."

He spoke quietly. "Stop it, Catherine. Don't do this."

Her smile was almost convincing. "The dance last night was lovely. Thanks so much for being my escort. My boss wants to put you on the payroll. He says you can squeeze money out of a stone."

He licked his lips. "What's wrong, honey?"

She bent and picked a dead leaf from one of the bushes, then straightened. "I'd offer you breakfast, but I haven't been to the store. Thanks for stopping by, Phillip. I'd better get back to my chores. You know how Saturdays are."

He took a step toward her, and she flinched. It hurt more than he thought possible. He cleared his throat. "Do I owe you an apology, Catherine? Did I offend you? Did I cause you pain?"

Her face went blank, and she wrapped her arms around her waist. "Of course not."

He held out his hands, his pride less important than this woman who was so clearly torn and troubled. "Please talk to me, sweetheart. Tell me why you were gone when I woke up."

She was so pale he feared she might faint. He hated pushing her, but this was too important to back away. He sighed. "Why, Catherine? Tell me why."

She looked down at the ground. "You took off my mask," she muttered.

He frowned. "I wanted you to be comfortable enough to sleep well. I'm sorry."

Her lips trembled. "The mask was a fantasy. The princess was a fantasy."

Light began to dawn, and for a moment, hope returned. He spoke gently. "That woman in the mask was you, Catherine. You're the one who made love to me and turned my world upside down."

She shook her head violently, agitation in every line of her body.

He continued doggedly, trying not to be dismayed by her body language. "I know who I held in my arms, Catherine. I remember whose breasts I touched, whose body I claimed. She was no fantasy princess. She was a flesh-and-blood woman."

He went closer, carefully taking her by the shoulders. She was so stiff, she might break if he said the wrong word. He kissed her forehead. "Mask or no mask, that wonderfully sensuous, infinitely sexy, amazingly beautiful woman was you, Catherine. Is you . . ."

Her careful mask of composure shattered, and he saw the anguish that darkened her eyes. "N-n-no," she cried. "Sh-sh-she's not."

Horror flashed across her face, and she clapped her hands over her mouth. Tears glistened in her eyes.

He gathered her into his arms. "What is it, honey?" She was so upset, she was having trouble talking.

Her nose was buried in his chest, and when she finally managed to answer him, her voice was muffled. "You were my fantasy, Phillip. One night, that's all. And the mask enabled me to be who I wanted to be."

She sniffled, and he handed her a handkerchief from his pocket with a deep sigh. "You're out of luck, then."

She pulled back, her damp lashes spiked, her blue eyes reflecting the morning sky. "What do you mean?"

He released her reluctantly as she blew her nose and stepped away, putting three feet between them.

He shrugged. "One night is not enough. Neither is one week, one month, or one year. I'm thirty-five years old, Catherine. I've waited a hell of a long time for the woman who will knock my feet out from under me. Now I've found her, and I'm not letting go. I love you."

If the hankie had been paper, she would have shredded it

to bits by now. "You don't understand," she said, her voice low. "I'm not like that, Phillip. I'm boring and conventional and unexciting. I have nothing in common with your princess."

He grinned. "You look a lot like her."

She seemed torn between despair and hope. "She wore a mask, Phillip. You've made a mistake."

He narrowed the space between them and touched the top button at her throat. "Let's see if I did."

Slowly, deliberately, he opened the shell buttons one at a time until her blouse hung loose. He slipped it from her shoulders and draped it over a bush. He removed her bra without ceremony and cupped her breasts in his palms.

With a single fingertip he circled first one deep pink nipple and then the other. They tightened and furled. The silence in the garden was deafening save for their mingled ragged breathing.

He dropped to his knees and tasted one sweet crest. Catherine sucked in a breath. He loved the way her hands automatically rubbed his scalp when he did this.

He sucked harder, starved for the taste of her, feeling like it had been days instead of hours since he held her last. When the other breast had received the same attention, he rose and kissed her mouth.

She was resistant at first, rigid in his arms. He touched her cheek. "Kiss me, Catherine." After a long, sweet mating of tongues, he held her carefully, trying to be the gentleman she deserved. He sighed against her hair. "You taste like cinnamon."

"It was on my toast," she said primly, making him laugh.

He tipped up her chin, forcing her to meet his eyes. "I want to take you upstairs."

Her jerky nod was so long in coming, it stole his breath. Even bare from the waist up, her posture never faltered.

They walked hand in hand up the front steps, entering the house and locking the door behind them. Without speaking they mounted the stairs and walked to her bedroom. He wasn't surprised to find it neat as a pin.

The windows were open, and sheer lace curtains billowed in the morning breeze. He shut them deliberately. "I don't want you to be self-conscious if we get loud," he said, monitoring her response.

She went bright red.

He smiled. "Exactly."

Catherine stood in the center of the room, watching him like a plump parakeet faced with a starving cat.

He ignored her and undressed slowly, piling everything in her rocking chair. When he was bare-ass naked, he turned to face her. He couldn't do anything about his recalcitrant prick. It shouted his intentions, rearing thick and hard against his abdomen.

He held out his hands. "Catherine?"

She toed off her shoes and then approached him slowly, her teeth nibbling at her bottom lip. He took her palms and placed them on either side of his neck. Carefully, he unzipped her pants and helped her step out of them and her panties.

When their bare bodies touched, chest to chest, thigh to thigh, they both sighed. He could almost be content with holding her like this. Almost, but not quite.

Gently, he removed the clasp from her hair and tossed it aside. He fluffed the honey blond tresses. They fell just past her shoulders, and when he buried his face in the silky strands at her neck, he inhaled the fragrance of verbena and lime.

He cleared his throat. "No games today, Catherine. No masks, no fantasies. Agreed?"

She laid a hand over his heart, her other arm curled around his neck. "Yes, Phillip."

He hoped her docility was only temporary. He'd enjoyed her naughty resistance the night before.

He scooped her into his arms and carried her to the bed. With one hand, he separated the mosquito netting and swept back the covers. He set her down carefully, like the princess she was. Then he climbed in beside her and closed the gap in the transparent drape.

She lay beside him, not moving, her long-lashed eyes wide and wary.

His lips twitched. "This is an awfully sexy and romantic bed for a woman who claims to be boring and conventional."

He saw the muscles in her long slender throat move as she swallowed. "I like a firm mattress," she said, her breathy voice at odds with the prosaic words.

He brushed the pale curls covering her sex. "Firm is important," he said soberly. He took her hand and guided it to his engorged penis. When her fingers closed around him, he moaned. *Sweet holy heaven.*

Without any prompting from him, she stroked his cock, relieving his mind and torturing his body. He didn't want to have to cajole her into participating. He wanted whole-hearted enthusiasm.

A few moments later, his own enthusiasm threatened to escalate out of control. He grabbed her wrist. "Stop." The blood pounded in his veins.

He panted, his body demanding one course of action, while his brain struggled for oxygen and reason. He lifted her astride him, not yet joining their bodies. Catherine still looked self-conscious, and he was determined to wipe that hesitant look from her face.

He used his cock to rub against her, teasing her clitoris. She gasped, and her eyelids fluttered shut. He squeezed her hips. "Eyes open, Princess."

She gazed down at him, her tousled hair making her look like a wanton angel. "I thought you said no fantasies."

He stroked her again in exactly the same way. "It's not a fantasy," he said simply. "You *are* a princess, *my* princess."

Her pleased smile eased a bit of the tension binding him. He pressed his penis against her once again and then set up a rhythm. This time when her eyes closed, he didn't protest. Her teeth were buried in her bottom lip. Her pale dewy skin flushed pink.

She moved her hips and wriggled and tried to mount him, but his strength and determination defeated her. He continued to use his cock as a flesh-and-blood vibrator.

And it was working. Her breath came in harsh pants. She leaned back, and her hands rested on his knees.

When he could tell she was close, he used his thumb to ignite the flash point. She screamed and bore down on his hand. It took everything he had not to impale her then and there. He held her hips as she writhed and rode out the orgasm.

When she slumped to his chest, he played with her hair. He traced her ear. "You see why I shut the windows," he teased.

She punched his shoulder halfheartedly. "You're a monster."

"I'm hurt that you think so."

She lifted her hand. "You made me come with your hand when there was a perfectly wonderful erection just waiting to be discovered."

"Discovered?"

"Mapped, mounted, traced from stem to stern."

"Sounds like fun."

She scooted down his body and took him in her mouth without ceremony. "Expedition commencing," she muttered, her tongue circling the head of his penis with startling effect.

"God, Catherine . . ." he groaned. "Don't ever stop what you're doing."

She raked him with her teeth. "You're not the boss now," she said as she squeezed his balls gently. "You're in *my* hands."

She did something with her fingernails that made every

inch of his skin tighten. He groaned and thrust upward, feeling her lips at his scrotum. He shivered and clenched his fists in the covers.

Now she was kissing his balls and stroking his shaft in tandem. Black spots danced in front of his eyes. He tugged handfuls of her hair. "Come here," he said hoarsely. "Now."

She circled the base of his cock and squeezed. "Beg me, Phillip."

And he did. He cajoled, he pleaded, he promised the moon. And all the while she destroyed him with her creative, generous mouth.

When he knew he couldn't last a minute longer, he choked out one last plea. She straightened to her knees and looked down at him, her hands fondling her own breasts. "You want me, Phillip?" she asked softly.

"More than my next breath," he ground out, dazzled by her eroticism.

She knelt over him, offering a breast. He sucked it hungrily, his arms pulling her down. He aligned their bodies and surged upward, feeling his painfully erect cock slide deep into her hot, tight sheath.

Her muscles squeezed him, and he cursed. "Ride me, dammit. Show me, Catherine. Show me what you want, sweetheart."

His beautiful princess lifted her hips and plunged back down, wringing a cry from both of their throats. Then she set up a rhythm that dragged him along in a river of lust. He held back his climax as long as he could. He tried counting backward, but he got stuck on sixty-nine when he thought about what he wanted to do to her next. The carnal mental image destroyed him.

Hot fire streaked from his scrotum up his shaft to the head of his dick, and he exploded with a harsh shout of release. Again and again. Aftershock and aftershock. And when it was over he was ashamed to realize he didn't know if she had come again or not.

His legs felt rubbery and numb. His eyes burned, and his arms ached. One of her curls tickled his chin.

Her silence bothered him, though he'd never been a man to need pillow talk. He stroked her hair. "What are you thinking, honey?"

She yawned. "Isn't that supposed to be the woman's line?"

He pinched her ass. "Smart aleck." He lay there in her bed and wondered if he would get to stay. And then a thought struck him.

He nudged her. "Catherine . . . are you awake?"

She burrowed deeper into his chest. "Barely. You didn't let me get much sleep last night."

He chuckled. "I just had a mental breakthrough."

"Sounds painful."

"I'm serious. Have you noticed that whenever I start to make love to you, you quit being shy and turn into a sexpot? It's been that way since we first kissed that night after I took you to dinner."

Long silence on her end.

He persisted. "Catherine? It's true. You claim to be boring and conventional and inhibited, but when we get within two feet of each another and have physical contact, you go wild in my arms."

"And which Catherine do you prefer?" A man would have to be a fool not to hear the plea for reassurance.

"Both," he said promptly. "I love watching you out in public. Miss Prim and Proper. And knowing that all I have to do is touch your breast or kiss your lips and you flame so hot I can hardly hold you . . . God, Catherine, you're every man's fantasy."

She rolled to her side and propped her chin on her hand. "I could live with that."

She looked adorable . . . pleased and proud and maybe a bit smug.

He stroked the curve where her rib cage dipped to her narrow waist and flared again at her hip. And then he frowned. "That same night when we first kissed, you said you had made a promise about me. What was it . . . and to whom?"

She wrinkled her nose. "You know my friends Kallie and Gina?"

He nodded. "I've met them. I know Gina better than Kallie."

"Well, we all celebrated our twenty-ninth birthdays recently, and we made a pact."

"Go on."

She hesitated and sighed. "We agreed that in this next

year leading up to the big 3-0 we would all act on a secret hidden fantasy."

His eyebrows lifted. "And that involves me how?"

She rolled her eyes. "Don't play dumb. The masked ball. Last night on your boat. That was my fantasy. Seducing Phillip Trent."

He pursed his lips. "Doesn't seem fair to your friends."

She frowned. "Why on earth not?"

He shrugged. "I was predisposed to being seduced. It really didn't take any effort on your part. I caved like a house of sand."

She sat up, and he forced his eyes from her luscious breasts to her face. She crossed her legs pretzel style. "It was still my fantasy. And it was hard to ask you out, Phillip. It took lots of guts. I'm shy."

He studied her nude body. "Yeah, I noticed."

She lifted her knees to her chest and circled them with her arms. Now he couldn't see her breasts, but her bottom . . .

He cleared his throat. "So that was it, fantasy over?"

She looked confused. "Well, I suppose. I don't have to share all the gory details with them, at least not until our birthdays next year."

He linked his arms behind his head. His cock was beginning to come back to life. How could it not with a nude Catherine a couple of feet away? "So let me get this straight. You had a year to act out this fantasy, and you jumped on the task in less than a month?"

"Less than three weeks," she said, looking guilty.

He pasted an arrogant grin on his face, a look sure to push her buttons. "It sounds to me like you were more eager than scared. You wanted me bad, sweetheart. Admit it. You love me."

Predictably, her eyes narrowed, and her chin lifted. "I thought you were an attractive, intelligent man. One of many in Charleston."

He sat up and stifled a smile when Catherine's eyes drifted to his crotch and widened. He leaned forward and kissed her. "You wanted me bad. You love me," he chanted softly.

She tugged his head back for a second kiss. "I was scared to death," she insisted.

He tumbled her to her back and settled between her thighs. Being the considerate, helpful woman that she was, she wrapped her legs around his waist and wiggled her ass until he had no choice but to slide deep. "Damn, woman . . ." he groaned.

Her eyes shut. "You're a wonderful fantasy, Phillip Trent. I'm glad I didn't waste another eleven months. And yes, I love you."

He buried his face in her neck, thrusting slowly, trying to hold back the inevitable. With ragged breaths, his heart pounding, he ground out a question. "Do you want to know my fantasy?"

She whimpered a protest when he stopped moving.

"Catherine? Look at me. Do you want to know?"

She opened her eyes with a pout. "Do you always talk this much during sex?"

"Brat." He flexed his hips and chuckled when she gasped.

He was losing it fast, so he asked again. "Do you want to know?"

"Yes," she hissed, her cheeks flushed with color. Her eyes softened, and she smiled at him so sweetly, his heart contracted. "Tell me, Phillip. What's your hidden fantasy?"

He caressed her cheek. "Loving you, Princess. I found the chink in the castle wall, and this gardener is never letting you go." Then he moved inside her and claimed his lady one more time.

Skin Deep

One

Kallie Bradshaw absentmindedly cleaned a paintbrush as she pondered the benefits of procrastination. Five months ago she celebrated her twenty-ninth birthday. Five months ago she made a pact with her two best friends. Five months ago she promised to seduce the man of her dreams within the following year.

Was she nuts?

With a long-suffering sigh that no one was around to hear, she continued straightening and organizing her oils and brushes. Watercolor was her specialty, but she'd been working more and more in oils, trying to refine and improve her technique.

She'd just wrapped up an enormous canvas of underwater sea life. It was a commissioned piece, destined to hang on a wall of the lobby in a downtown insurance building. On the one hand, the fee for that single huge watercolor would keep her in groceries for several months. But on the other hand, it stung to know that the painting she spent days producing would probably blend, unnoticed, into the bustle of a big public area.

She shouldn't complain. To be supporting herself entirely by her art at such a young age was unusual. The handful of small gallery shows she'd done had turned out to be gratifying successes. There was really no reason for her current dissatisfaction . . . that is, unless she admitted the real truth.

There was nothing wrong with her career. Her professional life was going right according to plan. It was her personal life that was the pits. And it could all be blamed on cowardice and procrastination.

Even Catherine, shy, introverted Catherine, had wasted no time in fulfilling her part of the pact. Now Kallie's tall, lovely blond friend was sporting an engagement ring with a stone the size of the rock of Gibraltar.

And Kallie was thrilled for her. Really. But it was hard not to be a little envious in the presence of Catherine and Phillip. Phillip looked at his new fiancée as if he'd won the lottery, and Kallie had never seen Catherine so happy.

In truth, Catherine's portion of the pact had an unfair advantage. Catherine already knew going into things that Phillip was attracted to her. In Kallie's situation, the man in question regarded her as an amalgam of best bud and little sister. It was frustrating to say the least. And it didn't bode well for her plans.

She swept up a couple of dust bunnies on the scarred hardwood floor and then stood the broom in the corner with another loud, pitiful sigh. She couldn't put it off any longer. She had a man to seduce. And it wasn't getting any easier.

An hour later, she parked her car near the entrance to Donovan's Reef. Beau Donovan, owner and proprietor of the casually chic restaurant and bar, was also coincidentally the object of her most heated fantasies.

She saw him the moment she walked in, and she hovered near the door for a few minutes, just for the sheer enjoyment of watching him with impunity.

The tourist crowd would never know that the laughing man behind the bar was the owner. He was wearing jeans and a teal DONOVAN'S REEF T-shirt that was just tight enough to reveal washboard abs and muscular shoulders.

Beau was several inches over six feet. His lanky frame and tousled blond hair, combined with a killer smile and baby blue eyes, drew women in droves. They bought drinks just for the chance to sit near him and flirt shamelessly.

Kallie started to sigh again and stopped herself. This defeatist attitude had to go. She was a woman. Beau liked women. She had a chance. A small one, perhaps . . . but a chance.

She lifted her chin and walked to the bar section of the premises. It was only eleven. The lunch crowd hadn't poured in yet, and Beau didn't seem overly busy.

She clambered onto a bar stool, inwardly cursing her lack of stature. At five foot one, she was vertically challenged in many situations. All her life she had wanted to be as tall as the elegant Catherine. Beau winked at her and moments later came her way with a cherry Coke. He knew her preferences without asking.

He chucked her chin. "Hey, munchkin. How's it hangin'?"

She took a deep breath and frowned. "I'm not a child, Beau. I'm a full-grown woman." Well, you wouldn't know it to look at her cup size, but she couldn't do anything about her modest breasts short of surgery, and she was never going that route. Ever.

Beau blinked and held up his hands. "Whoa, cupcake. Ease up. Is this one of those PMS days when I'm supposed to stay out of your face?"

That was the trouble with longtime friends. They thought they could say whatever the hell they pleased. She resisted the urge to toss her drink in his face with dramatic flair. "No," she said through clenched teeth. "It's not. I'm merely pointing out that your short jokes are getting old."

He looked hurt. "It wasn't a short joke. It was a term of affection." He cocked his head, studying her with unnerving intensity. "I'm sorry. You're not a munchkin. You're a small, perfect woman."

He grinned, and she couldn't help smiling in return. It was impossible to stay miffed with Beau. He was one of the most easygoing men she knew, and he hadn't meant to be unkind. He was probably dumbfounded. She'd never before been sensitive about her height . . . or lack thereof.

She took a sip of her Coke as Beau turned away for a moment to give the rotund guy a few stools down another beer.

Then he was back. "You going with me to the game

tonight?" Savannah, just down the coast, had a minor league baseball team, and during the season Beau and Kallie and three of their buddies usually made it to a couple or three games each month. The trip was an easy drive from Charleston.

"Sure," she said casually. "I'm in. What about the guys?"

Beau shrugged. "They're all busy this evening. But I don't want to miss this game, so I'm glad you're up for it."

She nibbled her bottom lip and shifted a bowl of peanuts. "We could go out to dinner beforehand."

Beau frowned. "I thought we always got hot dogs at the game."

She wrinkled her nose, mentally conceding defeat. "You're right. Wouldn't want to miss that."

She spent the afternoon doing errands. Anytime she was in the midst of a project, she tended to check out of the real world for days at a time. Bananas rotted, bread got stale, and bills went unpaid. She was a bit obsessive about her art, and she had never mastered the knack of moderation. It wasn't unusual for her to keep painting until one or two in the morning when she was on a roll.

But eventually she had to surface, and when she did, playing catch-up was a bitch. Boring, sometimes overwhelming, but definitely necessary.

She had her hair trimmed and got a manicure and pedicure. That was a treat. Her fingernails were usually paint-stained and broken. Just once she wanted to look feminine, even if it was short-lived.

She even took the time to buy a new shirt. Okay . . . so it was a plain T-shirt just like a dozen others in her closet, but at least it was new and it was a pretty shade of coral and it didn't have any flecks of paint on it. She should get fashion points for that.

Although she'd go to her grave before she'd ever admit it, she bought a lot of her casual clothes in the largest youth size at the Gap. They fit her, and besides, she rarely needed anything more sophisticated.

When she absolutely had to have something for evening wear, she paid a visit to a very talented dressmaker who managed to make her look like a dressed-up woman as opposed to a little girl playing dress-up. It was a subtle but important difference.

After the self-beautification rituals, she bought groceries and cleaned her apartment, actually remembering to wear rubber gloves to save her manicure. Housework was way down on her list of favorite activities, but she had developed an efficient system that kept her away from her painting as short a time as possible.

In earlier days she had worked out of her home, but that had been a disaster. She had no sense of boundaries, no way to separate work from the rest of her life. Consequently, she'd painted feverishly from morning until night 24/7.

Catherine and Gina had done an intervention, and Kallie had then moved her studio to its present location. She had a comfy sofa there where she still tended to crash on occasion, but at least she tried to go home at the end of the day.

Other than her two best friends, Beau was the only person who had much success dragging her away from her painting. And that was because Beau knew and understood her other passion . . . baseball. Perhaps it was inevitable growing up in a house with three brothers, but she adored the game and all its nuances.

She was only eleven or twelve when her big, tough brothers began allowing her to tag along with them to games. They drove all over the Southeast to minor league play, and since they were die-hard Braves fans, Atlanta was the destination of choice for the majors.

It was on those outings that Kallie had gradually become "one of the guys." Her brothers' friends came and went . . . and occasionally as Kallie got older, one of the group would bring a girl along. But many times Kallie was the only female allowed in the all-male enclave.

When she was a senior in high school, she'd won a contest that allowed her to actually sit in the press box and visit the dugout at Turner Field. She still had a picture of herself interviewing Chipper Jones and Bobby Cox. The guys had all been green with envy.

Beau entered the mix when Kallie was at the very impressionable age of fifteen. His family wasn't nearly as wealthy as the Bradshaws, who owned a string of restaurants up and down the southeast coast. But his parents had scrimped and saved to send him to private school, and he had been a classmate of Kallie's middle brother.

Her three siblings were all married now and had moved away from Charleston, but Beau remained, and their little group had expanded with the addition of a trio of Beau's fraternity brothers.

It was pretty much an exercise in self-torture for Kallie to tag along these days. Having Beau's camaraderie and nothing more was depressing. But spending time with him was something she couldn't give up, no matter how futile or hopeless her crush.

She usually met Beau and the guys at the restaurant. But since it was just the two of them tonight, Beau had suggested taking his new car . . . a vintage black Porsche with cream interior.

He pulled up in front of her apartment at five on the dot. She had been watching out the window, and she hurried down the steps and met him before he could get out. Having Beau near her bed was too much of a temptation. She didn't trust herself not to pounce on him and force him to have sex with her. And it might come to that if her other plan didn't work.

He flicked her ponytail and kissed her cheek when she got in. He was an affectionate guy, and it wasn't unusual for him to give her a bear hug.

The car's interior was small and intimate. Beau's aftershave scented the air, and she could tell he had been home to shave and shower. His khaki shorts were wrinkled but clean. Her heart beat faster at such close proximity. A more sensual woman would have known how to begin the seduction routine.

Kallie racked her brain for a sexy move, but after each

scenario in her mental Rolodex seemed more goofy than the last, she finally gave up and sat back to enjoy the trip.

Beau kept one eye on the road and one on Kallie. He had paid each of his friends a hundred bucks to back out of tonight's trip and keep their mouths shut about the financial arrangement. He wanted Kallie to himself in a non-threatening environment. He knew she considered him one of her best friends along with Catherine and Gina, and frankly . . . friendship sucked.

It had taken him a long time to realize that his feelings for Kallie were more than platonic. Okay, so maybe he wasn't the sharpest tool in the shed. When he first felt a stirring of interest in his petite buddy, he'd been horrified. Her three brothers would have castrated him and tossed him in the ocean if they had ever guessed. So he had shoved all those interesting feelings in a locked box and thrown away the key.

But as the years passed, he opened the box from time to time, and the feelings got stronger. He tried avoiding the potentially disastrous fascination. But Kallie was not so easily ignored. She might be small, but she packed a punch. Her big brown eyes could stop a man in his tracks. She had beautiful chestnut hair that was naturally curly. Kallie hated it, but he'd had a number of fantasies about that hair.

When she hopped into the car tonight, he almost swallowed his tongue. She was wearing cutoff denim overalls, and they were damned short. She had a light, pretty tan. Her slender, nicely toned arms and legs were bare. A tank top was the only visible piece of clothing beneath the overalls, and for the life of him, he couldn't see a bra strap.

He kept his attention on the road, trying to keep track of the conversation. Maybe this alone thing wasn't such a good idea. He and Kallie were never at a loss for something to talk about, but now that he had admitted to himself that he wanted Kallie as more than just a friend, he felt awkward and jittery.

She leaned her seat back and propped her feet on the dash. She'd ditched her little flat sandals the moment she got in the car. Kallie didn't do shoes unless it was absolutely necessary.

He sneaked a sideways glance at her narrow feet. Her toes were painted fire-engine red, and her small, oval fingernails matched perfectly. Her hands rested on her bare thighs. He imagined those glossy nails raking gently down his erection . . . closing around him and sliding up and down.

Whoa, Donovan. Get a grip. He wiped a shaky hand across his forehead. Kallie was humming along to a song on the radio while he was imploding. Even if he was planning to ease her into a more "romantic" relationship, he couldn't dissolve into a blithering idiot in the meantime. He needed to keep things on an even keel. At least until he figured out how to handle the sexual feelings that were keeping him awake at night.

He wasn't exactly sure how to broach the subject. How did you tell a woman you'd known since she wore braces that you wanted to jump her bones?

It required a certain amount of finesse, and he wasn't at

all sure that finesse was in his repertoire. Finesse was more Phillip Trent's style. Trent was a sophisticated man of the world. Phillip probably took Catherine to fine French restaurants. Beau much preferred the beer and hot dogs at a ball game.

So maybe finesse was out. But if he wanted Kallie, he had to segue from sharing a love of baseball to sharing another sport that was more one-on-one and infinitely more exciting.

They made it to the small stadium in just less than two hours. Kallie tucked a lip gloss and some folded bills in her pocket, and he locked her purse in the trunk. He carried his lucky glove.

They squabbled at the ticket window. "I'm buying your ticket," he said firmly. Though everybody usually went dutch on these outings, he wanted tonight to seem more like a date. The crowd was pretty big, but they were able to get seats along the first-base line.

He bought hot dogs and chips, a beer for him, and a Coke for Kallie. She didn't drink alcohol very often. She was so small that a little bit made her loopy.

When they were in their seats and listening to the announcer run through the lineups, he relaxed. This was comfortable. He could quit being so freaked out in this environment.

They finished their food and discussed the merits of the starting pitchers. Kallie had a sharp, analytical mind, and she understood and appreciated the game as much or more than any guy he knew.

Kallie may have considered herself a tomboy growing up, but she had matured into a beautiful, sexy woman. When he was sitting beside her, sometimes with an arm looped across the back of her chair, the game didn't hold his attention nearly as much as it used to.

It didn't escape his notice that Kallie seemed fidgety this evening. She was normally into the game from the moment the umpire yelled, "Play ball!" But tonight, her attention was everywhere . . . on a cute toddler a few seats over, on the teenage couple necking behind them, on the players standing beside the dugout just in front of them.

In all fairness, the game was not going all that well for the Savannah Sand Gnats. Play-off season was fast approaching, which was why Beau had particularly wanted to see this matchup. But Savannah, who was supposed to win, was falling apart. If he'd been a superstitious guy, it might have worried him.

At the end of the third inning, a light misty rain started to fall. A nuisance, but not enough to stop the game. It only made things more hot and muggy. He was wearing a short-sleeve cotton shirt unbuttoned over a T-shirt, so he shrugged out of it and handed it to Kallie, hoping it would at least keep her dry. She leaned forward, and he held first one of her arms and then the other to maneuver them into the sleeves.

Kallie shivered as Beau's big warm hands touched her casually. She wasn't cold, but the shirt still held his body heat and his smell, and she wrapped it around her with an inward smile of pleasure. Maybe she could take the soft garment home and keep it. Like some lovesick high school girl.

Sitting beside Beau Donovan at a baseball game was something she had done a million times. And she'd never once let on that being so close to him affected her sexually. She'd been calm, casual, and friendly. But knowing what she was getting ready to propose made her legs quivery, even sitting down.

Every time she visualized actually saying the words out loud, her nipples tightened, her pulse accelerated, and her breathing got ragged. A Valium sounded good right about now.

Beau was oblivious. He was good-naturedly heckling the first baseman for the other team. It was fun to watch Beau at a baseball game. He got so worked up. She imagined that same passion transferred over to the bedroom.

Thinking about Beau Donovan in bed only made her nervous physical symptoms that much worse. From time to time over the last few years, she'd been forced to endure the sight of Beau with one pretty woman or another. He seemed to prefer blondes, but then what man didn't? And the women he usually dated were tall. Which helped, since Beau was almost six four.

So why did she think there was any chance he would be attracted to short, flat-chested, and dark?

It wasn't like she wanted to marry the guy. *Liar,* her subconscious screamed. She just wanted to satisfy her curiosity and make good on a pact with her friends. She was playing out a fantasy . . . that's all. Making a dream come true. Seducing Beau Donovan for one night of incredible, magical, sweaty, wonderful sex.

"You want another Coke?"

She jumped about a foot when Beau touched her arm. "No, thanks. I'm fine."

He looked at her oddly, but got up and climbed across her legs to go to the concession stand. She couldn't sit still. She escaped to the restroom and stared in the mirror. Her eyes looked panicked . . . almost wild. Her hair was corkscrewing in the increased humidity, and her lips were pale.

She pulled out her lip gloss and with a shaky hand applied a coat of soft rosy color. She rested her palms on the sink and bent her head, taking deep breaths. What's the worst thing that could happen? Beau might be horrified and embarrassed, and their friendship would be ruined forever.

God, when she laid it out like that, it sounded far too risky. But the pact with Catherine and Gina was serious. She'd given her word. It was more than just whimsy. It was a pledge to live life to the fullest.

Which led her right back to where she'd been that morning . . . acknowledging her own pathetic cowardice and procrastination.

Okay . . . here was the plan. If Savannah scored a home run in the bottom of the fourth inning, she would take it as a positive sign. And given the way things were going, she should be safe for tonight. Then she could go home and rethink this crazy plan.

When she got back, Beau was already in his seat. He took his eyes off the field for a split second. "I thought you disappeared."

"Pit stop," she said casually, gripping the arms of the seat to keep her hands from shaking.

Beau shouted as the newest Savannah batter hit a double, advancing the runner on first base to third. The next guy up, a power hitter, was intentionally walked. Bases loaded.

Kallie relaxed. There were two outs already, and the guy at the plate had a dismal batting average. He'd barely gotten a base hit this season. A newspaper columnist had called it the slump of the century. The poor batter's last home run was sometime in 2005.

The pitcher was being extra careful. No way could he walk this batter. The first pitch was a strike, high and inside. The batter let it go by. The second pitch was right down the middle. A swing and a miss. The third pitch was high and almost outside, but still in the strike zone. The bat connected with a loud crack, and the ball went sailing deep into center and over the wall.

The home crowd went wild. Beau was on his feet cheering. Kallie stood up automatically, numb with shock. The fates or the universe or some cosmic baseball karma had given her a clear signal. She couldn't back out.

When the furor settled and the game progressed, she sat there stunned. She thought about calling Gina for moral support, but her cell phone was in the car. It took two more innings to work up her nerve.

She said his name. "Beau?"

He was distracted, his attention on the field. "Hmmm?" The game was close, and the other team had a big hitter at bat.

"Beau?" She didn't really mind that he wasn't looking at her. It made things a fraction easier.

"What, Kallie?" Still looking at the field.

"Will you pose for me in the nude so I can paint you?" She blurted it out and felt her stomach do a free fall.

His head snapped around so fast, it was a wonder his neck didn't break. "What did you say?"

She tried to smile, but her lips wouldn't move. "I want to paint you in the nude," she whispered.

His expression was stunned, his eyes hazy and wide. He opened his mouth. "I, uh . . ."

At that exact moment, a foul ball sailed into the seats in Section 103 and clonked Beau Donovan on the temple.

Two

Beau slumped forward into her arms, out cold. Two kids bumped her knees as they scrambled beneath the seats for the loose ball.

Rational thought abandoned her as she tried to support two hundred plus pounds of unconscious male. Her heart was in her throat. A huge knot was rising already from the point of impact, and a nasty purplish-red bruise marred the skin at his hair line.

"Beau," she cried frantically. "Beau . . . are you okay?"

Beau was definitely not okay. Paramedics were on the scene in a heartbeat, easing her out of the way and gently lifting Beau onto a stretcher. His face was pale, and she gazed at his chest urgently to see if he was breathing. Head wounds could be fatal.

She trailed after the little caravan of medical personnel, following them down the sideline to the small tent where an ambulance was parked. They loaded him in and wouldn't let her ride. She had to fish his keys from his pocket and race to an exit, all the while clutching Beau's not-so-lucky glove to her chest.

Beau's car was a straight shift, and she ground the gears twice before she was able to ease out of the parking space. She kept one eye on the ambulance. She didn't know a soul in Savannah, and if she got lost on the way to the hospital, it would cost her precious minutes.

It gave her some hope that the ambulance didn't have its siren on. It was driving rapidly, but not careening between lanes, so once they got off the stadium property, she didn't have any problems keeping up.

The hospital ended up being about twenty minutes away. She parked under a streetlight in the lot closest to the emergency entrance, locked the Porsche carefully, and ran inside to the ER waiting area.

It was another hour before they let her go back to see him. When she spotted the empty cubicle, her vision went fuzzy around the edges.

The attending nurse was kind. "They've taken him up for a CT scan. You're welcome to sit here until he gets back."

It was the longest sixty minutes of her life. By the time an orderly rolled Beau's bed back into place and got him settled, Kallie was a wreck. She stood hovering until the man left, and then she approached the bed.

Beau lay perfectly still, an IV hooked to his arm, his face frighteningly pale. "Beau?" She said his name softly, afraid to touch him.

His eyelids fluttered and opened. He attempted a smile.

"Hey, munchkin. Can you beg them for drugs? I've got a bitch of a headache."

Her bottom lip trembled. She leaned over the bed and carefully smoothed his hair. "You scared the crap out of me, Donovan. And no . . . I don't think they'll let you take anything until the doctor reads the CT scan."

She took a small cloth from the table and wet it with water from a pitcher. The pitcher had ice in it, so the water was cold. She placed it across his forehead, avoiding his scary-looking bump.

Beau groaned and moved restlessly in the bed.

"Too cold?" she said anxiously.

The crease between his brows deepened. "No. But I feel sick."

Kallie buzzed for a nurse and stroked Beau's hand while they waited.

An older woman swished the curtain aside and took a look at the patient with a pleasant grin. "I heard you tangled with a baseball and lost."

Beau grunted, his face tight. The nurse inserted a syringe in the IV. "The doctor says you have a concussion. He'll be in to talk to you in a few minutes. This should help the nausea and the pain."

As quickly as she had come, the woman disappeared again.

It was more like a half hour before the harried doctor finally made an appearance. He was all business, but he answered Kallie's questions patiently. "He was only unconscious for a little while. All the tests look good. It's not really necessary to admit him, though since you're from out of town, I'd suggest spending the night in a nearby motel."

Kallie nodded. "No problem. What do I need to do during the night?"

"You'll want to wake him every couple of hours as a precaution, at least until morning. If he's lucid each time, you can let him go right back to sleep. As long as he improves steadily, he needn't come back here. His own doctor can give him a checkup in four or five days. Don't be alarmed if he's irritable. And he may not remember the moments right before and right after the accident. That's normal."

Kallie murmured her gratitude and slipped out to deal with paperwork. Fortunately, Beau's insurance card was in his billfold, so that took care of most everything. Thankfully, the ER wasn't too busy that night. A helpful nurse made a suggestion about lodging, so Kallie called and lined up a room, grimacing when the only one available was a king.

She went back inside just long enough to let Beau know what was going on, and then brought the car up to the covered portico.

Another orderly pushed Beau's wheelchair out. The Beau she knew would have protested being ferried around like an invalid. The fact that he didn't argue at all worried her.

The hotel where she had made a reservation was two blocks away. Beau's eyes were closed, and she couldn't tell if he was awake or not.

She pulled into a twenty-minute check-in spot. "Beau?" She tapped his arm.

"Hmmm?" His eyes were still closed.

"Do I need to get someone to help us inside?"

He frowned and straightened in his seat with a groan. When he opened his eyes, they were hazy and unfocused. He shook his head and cursed as the instinctive motion clearly made his head throb. "No. I can do it."

Kallie hesitated, not sure he was capable of making decisions at this point. But she was afraid if she told him she was going to get assistance, he might try to follow her on his own to prove a point. So she agreed reluctantly. "Okay, then. Sit tight. I'll be right back."

She went inside and registered as quickly as possible, also making arrangements for a bellman to park the car. When she went back outside, she opened Beau's door and roused him with a hand on his shoulder. "Come on, big guy. Let's get you up to bed."

He staggered a bit as he stood up, but he made it onto the elevator and up to their room without incident.

He stood by the bed and looked around as though lost. She touched his elbow. "Do you need help getting undressed?" The question came out calm and even, but her insides were shaking.

He frowned. "I'm gonna take a shower."

She shook her head, and it was her turn to frown. "You'd better not. If you pass out, I won't be able to get you up off the floor."

He thrust out his chin, a mulish look in his eyes. "Back off, short stuff. You're not my mother."

She winced. The doc hadn't been kidding about the

irritability thing. She hovered near the bathroom as he disappeared inside and closed the door in her face. She heard the water turn on and then a series of curses. Probably from trying to get his shirt off over his head. She was worried sick, but she couldn't bring herself to intrude on his privacy.

When she heard the water finally turn off, she hurried toward the bed, carefully folding back the covers on the nearest side. Beau appeared in the doorway moments later, and her heart jumped into her throat and then plummeted to her stomach. He was nude.

Well, almost. A miniscule hotel towel wrapped around the hips of a six-foot-four-inch male didn't leave a lot to the imagination.

She cleared her throat. "You'd better lie down."

He was practically swaying on his feet. His hair was damp, and droplets of water still clung to his broad shoulders.

He made it across the room and, before her very eyes, dropped the towel without ceremony and sprawled on his back on the king-size bed with all his hitherto unseen parts on full display.

She tried not to stare . . . she really did. But sweet holy hannah. The man was a god. A really well-endowed god. A poster boy for virility.

Fortunately, he didn't notice her drooling deer-in-the-headlights look. His eyes were firmly closed, and his forehead was squinched up in pain.

She pulled the covers over him, wishing she could use a hot room as an excuse to leave him as he was. But the air-conditioning was functioning with annoying efficiency. As she smoothed the comforter over his chest, he muttered something.

She leaned closer. "What is it, Beau? I didn't hear you."

He put a tentative hand to his temple, his lips pressed together in a thin line. "Can I have something for this god-awful headache?"

She glanced at her watch and winced. "I can give you something else in half an hour. I'm sorry. Try to sleep." The nurse had given them enough medicine to last until they could get a prescription filled the next day.

He slipped into a fitful doze, and she took a turn in the bathroom. She rinsed out her panties and hung them up to dry. She hadn't worn a bra. Her barely-there boobs didn't need much support, and beneath the denim overalls, it hadn't seemed necessary.

She took a quick shower and slipped back into Beau's long-sleeve shirt. It hung below her knees, and the cotton was soft enough to be comfortable for a night's sleep. Exhaustion was catching up with her, making her body feel heavy and uncoordinated. She yearned for the oblivion of a deep, dreamless sleep, but that wouldn't happen tonight since she'd have to wake him periodically. Just before she climbed into bed, she set the alarm on her watch.

She leaned toward his side of the bed and studied him. In repose, he seemed younger, more vulnerable. He was quiet and still, and some of the pain lines had eased from his forehead. Maybe he was resting comfortably. She hoped so. Seeing him unconscious and in pain had shredded her heart into a million aching pieces.

She turned off the light and slid beneath the covers, leaving a good four feet between her and temptation. She had cut the AC back, but the room still felt chilly. A really desperate and amoral woman might have curled up against the big, warm male who lay so conveniently close, but Kallie had a few scruples left.

In the dark, the situation felt even more intimate. She could hear him breathing. She could smell the dizzying scent of soap and male skin. She scooted a bit and reached out a hand to touch his ribs. Fear for his safety still hovered in her mind, but she was reassured by the steady rise and fall of his chest.

She roused him to take his medicine, and then, with a sigh, she returned to her side of the bed and finally drifted off to sleep.

Beau surfaced slowly, groaning in disbelief. He'd never been one to abuse alcohol, even in his college days, but he was in the grip of a powerful hangover. Nausea made his stomach pitch and roll, and a dagger of pain sliced into his temple. "Shit," he hissed as he tried to sit up and fell back, shivering helplessly like a damned baby. He needed to pee, but he wasn't sure he could even make it to the bathroom.

He flinched when a light clicked on and a small hand touched his forehead. "Take it easy, Beau. Do you need some water?"

"Kallie?" Her soft voice was comforting and familiar. What was Kallie doing in his bedroom? Oh, lord. Had he done something stupid?

He turned his head slowly. She hovered over him anxiously, her tousled hair falling around her cheeks. Her brown eyes were dark with concern. She smoothed his brow. "Do you remember what happened?"

He searched his decidedly nonfunctional brain and came up blank. Flashes of memory danced near and away with annoying capriciousness. He tried to concentrate. "The hospital?"

She nodded, seeming relieved. "You were hit in the head with a baseball."

"We went to see the Sand Gnats play," he muttered, struggling to make sense of things.

"Yeah."

"Why didn't I catch it?"

Her eyes widened into a panicked expression, and then she bent her head. "You were distracted."

He gave up trying to think that one through. Too much effort. He rolled to his side. "Gotta go to the bathroom," he mumbled. He tried to sit up and then ground out a series of curses as his head protested.

Kallie scooted out of bed and ran around to his side. "Careful. Let me help you."

He was in too much pain to be embarrassed. He got to his feet slowly, trying to suck it up and be a man. But sweet Jesus, his head hurt. He swayed, and Kallie's arm came around his waist. He doubted whether she'd be able to handle him if he went out cold, but he was glad of the support anyway.

Her slender arm felt good against his bare skin. They

made it to the bathroom in about six steps, and he pushed her aside gently. "I've got this covered," he muttered, trying to smile but failing.

When he had taken care of business, he shuffled back to the bedroom and allowed his little nurse to tuck him back in bed. The pillow cradled his aching head. "Drugs?" he asked hopefully.

She shook her head. "I'm sorry. Forty-five more minutes."

He groaned and closed his eyes, trying to brace himself against the thud of his heartbeat in his temples. If she'd had a sledgehammer, he'd get her to put him out of his misery.

Her lips grazed his forehead. "Try to sleep," she whispered. He clung to her voice as he slid into a medicated doze once again.

The night seemed a million years long. Every five minutes it seemed, Kallie woke him up and kept asking him stupid questions. What was his name? What was her name? Where did he work?

Finally, he protested. "If you have an ounce of compassion in your body, you'll let me sleep, dammit." He heard her sigh and felt instantly guilty.

She supported his head and helped him swallow two more tablets with a swig of water from a glass tumbler. The faint light of dawn was leaking into the room, and Kallie looked about as bad as he felt.

Her eyes were troubled. "You can rest now," she said softly. "I'll leave you alone."

As the medicine slowly kicked in, he stretched restlessly. He was cold and exhausted, and so miserable he wanted to cry like a baby. He turned on his side and reached for Kallie. He felt her go perfectly still when his hand touched her hip.

He pulled her into his embrace, ignoring her sputtered protests, and tucked her against his chest, circling an arm beneath her breasts. "Be still," he murmured, absorbing her warmth and softness with a shiver of delight. "Go to sleep, honey."

At the back of his mind, he was aware of something not quite right, something niggling at his conscience, but he was too far gone to care. He nuzzled her hair, kissed the back of her neck, and slid into oblivion.

To her amazement, Kallie slept. Deeply, peacefully, like she was the one drugged.

Sleeping wasn't the difficult part. It was the waking up that was a bitch. Her heart stopped in panic and then restarted with a sluggish thump.

Her shirt, or Beau's shirt to be exact, was tucked up around her waist. His nude body was plastered to hers, and an impressive erection nestled against her butt cheeks. This wasn't quite how she envisioned the two of them in bed together, but it was pretty darned good.

Of course if he woke up, there would be hell to pay. With no small amount of regret, she tried to lift his heavy arm and slip free.

Beau muttered and moved restlessly in his sleep. His arm tightened like a steel band around her waist. His penis flexed and thickened.

She breathed raggedly, choking back a bubble of hysteria. She craned her neck for a peek at the digital clock. It was only seven thirty. The DO NOT DISTURB sign was on the door. No one was around to comment on her lack of moral fiber. And she wasn't precisely seducing an incapacitated man. She was merely enjoying a morning cuddle.

With that masterful piece of rationalization in place, she pillowed her head on his forearm and closed her eyes once again.

Beau wondered how it was possible for the two halves of a man's body to experience such a terrible dichotomy. From the waist down, he was in heaven. His throbbing dick was tucked up against a soft, warm ass. It was amazing. But when he contemplated even the most gentle of thrusts, his brain screamed at him in disbelief.

His head felt like someone had taken a baseball bat to it while he slept. Hammers pounded inside his skull, and only by remaining perfectly still was he able to keep from moaning.

Kallie stirred in his embrace, and his arms tightened around her. He probably should be able to remember how she came to be in his bed, but right now he didn't give a shit. Right now her amazing body was the only thing keeping him sane.

The ache in his cock intensified. Maybe just a little bit. He rearranged their bodies a hair, and now his prick slid between her sleek thighs. Not penetrating her, just rubbing back and forth.

He heard her breath catch in her throat. He cupped her sweet, delicate breast and heard her whimper. He pulled and tugged at her nipple, feeling it peak beneath his fingertips. "God, Kallie." He bit the side of her neck, his entire body tensing as a wave of lust swept over him.

She was trembling in his arms. She half turned to face him, shoving her hair from her face. "We can't do this, Beau. You'll hurt yourself." Her earnest expression touched something deep inside him. Her soft heart was one of the things he loved most about her

He kissed her lips softly. "Hurts anyway," he mumbled, trying to ignore the pounding, relentless agony in his head. He avoided contemplating what an orgasm would do to exacerbate that.

She lifted a hand to his cheek, stroking the stubble and making him weak. "Please, Beau. Be reasonable. You need to sleep. Please."

He'd always tried his best to do anything Kallie asked of him. And sleep was dragging him back under anyway. He groaned and tried to ignore everything below the waist. "Okay," he grumbled, settling back into his pillow. "But only because I want to be able to give you my best game." He thought he heard her laugh nervously, but he faded out before he could be sure.

When he awoke the next time he was alone. He blinked and stretched, slowly assessing his surroundings. This wasn't his bedroom. He turned his head gingerly. The pain had subsided to moderate discomfort. He scanned the room, looking for clues.

Nothing. He remembered a wheelchair and the hotel lobby. And he remembered a long string of disturbing dreams. But beyond that, a blank.

He was nude beneath the sheets. His stomach growled, and he realized he was starving. He eased into a sitting position, trying not to jar his head more than necessary. He heard the sound of a key in the lock, and he barely had time to jerk the sheet to his waist before Kallie slipped into the room carrying a bucket of ice.

Her eyes widened when she saw him, but she recovered quickly. "You're awake."

He scrubbed a hand over his face. "Yeah."

She set the container on the dresser and approached him, stopping at the foot of the bed. Her eyes dropped briefly to his bare chest before returning to his face and studying him with such intensity he had to fight the urge to squirm. "What?" he asked grumpily.

Her lips quirked. "How do you feel?"

"Like I tangled with a bottle of Jack Daniel's and lost."

She wrinkled her nose. "No alcohol involved. Do you remember what happened?"

He closed his eyes, trying to get hold of the feathery images that teased him. The effort made him sweat, but he emerged triumphant. "We were at a ball game." He felt absurdly grateful to have that much, at least.

She nodded. "You got hit in the head with a foul ball." Her answer seemed strangely familiar. Had she told him that before?

He frowned, his pride stung. "Why didn't I try to catch it?"

The flush of color in Kallie's cheeks deepened to a rosy pink. Her posture was wary. "I told you this earlier—you must have been distracted."

She looked so guilty that alarm bells went off in his head. He narrowed his eyes, trying to remember. But knowing that he was completely nude and having Kallie watch him so intently did weird things to his libido. And then it hit him. Why he'd been so unaware of what was happening on the field. Why Kallie looked so uneasy.

He remembered her request.

And when he did, he saw in her face that she knew he knew. Her gaze darted away from his. She locked her arms around her waist.

The temperature in the room went up about ten degrees, and his cock stirred. No wonder the stupid ball knocked him senseless. Kallie's artless question had knocked the breath out of him in another way.

She was pale now. Anxious. Uneasy. She twisted her hands at her waist. "I've ordered a bunch of stuff from room service. I thought you might be hungry. I didn't know what you'd want, so I pretty much asked for some of everything. The doctor said you could have whatever you felt like eating.

We've got one more dose of medicine to help you make the trip home, and then we'll have to get the prescription filled as soon as we get there. I called the restaurant. Phil said for you not to worry. He's got everything covered. I told him you'd be out for a couple of days at least. I tried to—"

He interrupted her babbling run-on sentences. "Calm down, Kallie." He saw her swallow.

"I'm calm," she insisted.

"Come here."

She was rooted to the spot.

He held out his hand. "Come here."

Her continued resistance pissed him off. Visions of holding her breast, teasing her pert nipple, made him crazy. Was it a dream or an actual memory?

He hated being at such a disadvantage. What the hell had happened in this bed last night? Everything converged to give him the surly temper of a starving bear just waking up from hibernation.

His arm dropped. He grabbed a handful of sheet and flipped it back, revealing every inch of his body to Kallie's stunned gaze. "Got a paintbrush handy?" he asked with a snarl.

Three

She choked out a protest and fled, letting the door slam behind her with a thud that reverberated in his head with nauseating consequences.

Well, hell. Perhaps that wasn't the smartest move he'd ever made. He stood up and headed for the bathroom, reasonably sure she wouldn't be back in the next five minutes. He found his clothes and dressed, carefully curbing his movements to avoid starting up the bongo drums inside his skull.

He looked in the mirror and winced. The side of his skull where the ball had hit him was a nasty mess of raw, scraped skin and colorful bruising. He probed gently at the knot and hissed in pain. Better to leave that alone. At least he wasn't nauseous anymore.

His stomach growled, reminding him that he hadn't eaten in hours. A loud knock drew him back to the bedroom. He checked the peephole and opened the door. The waiter rolled in a tray that was overflowing with silver dishes.

He started to remove the covers, but Beau stopped him. "Just leave it. Thanks." Beau reached for his pocket to tip the guy and realized belatedly that he had no clue where his billfold was.

He felt his cheeks flush, but the man took pity on him. "The lady took care of it, sir. Enjoy your breakfast."

Beau glanced at the clock as the door closed. Breakfast was stretching it. Almost lunch by now. And where was Kallie? He should wait for her, but hunger was making him dizzy. He dragged the desk chair close to the cart and began uncovering the bounty.

The smell alone was enough to make him weak. He dug in, sure that Kallie would return any moment. He was on his third cup of coffee when she finally reappeared.

His hand froze in midsip. He lowered the cup slowly and set it down with a little clink in the saucer. "Where have you been?"

She flinched. Perhaps the question had come out more harshly than he intended. He tempered his voice. "I saved you some food."

When it became clear that she wasn't willing to join him, he got up and went to the bed, picking up the remote and feigning interest in the TV just so she would eat. While he flipped channels, he watched her.

She nibbled at a piece of toast and ate two slices of bacon. She skipped the coffee and made herself a cup of tea. Kallie had spent a semester in London during her junior year in college, and she had picked up the habit then. She claimed it relaxed her.

Which posed the question . . . why was Kallie tense? He snorted inwardly. Perhaps because her best male friend had lewdly flashed her after she spent an entire restless night caring for his sorry butt?

Shame washed over him. He owed her an apology. But for some odd reason, he was having a hell of a time responding to her normally. He kept having flashes of Kallie's pretty, warm breast cupped in his palm. And her firm white ass pillowing his rock-hard prick. All of which was surely nothing more than a delicious wet dream . . . right?

Oh, they had shared a bed, sure. But the damned thing was big enough for five people. Knowing Kallie, she had kept to her side religiously. Hadn't she?

Why couldn't he remember?

He glanced at the clock again. The room that had felt like a cozy retreat from reality now felt like a prison. If he didn't get out of here soon, he was in danger of doing something highly inappropriate. Concussion or no concussion.

He cleared his throat. "Shouldn't we have had to check out by now?"

She slanted him a look. "I paid extra to stay until three. I wasn't sure if you'd be ready to get up this morning."

It was a perfectly innocent statement. No reason at all for his cock to rise to attention. He shifted on the bed, unobtrusively trying to adjust his jeans.

From this angle he could study the innocent curve of the back of her neck. She had pulled her hair up into a ponytail, and again he felt a flash of something . . . he had tasted that neck. He was sure of it.

A pulse began to beat low in his scrotum. The hunting instinct kicked in. Had he or had he not experienced carnal knowledge of Kallie Bradshaw? He closed his eyes, straining to recall last night. Warm thighs. He remembered sliding his erect cock back and forth between warm thighs.

He shuddered and groaned. Kallie leapt to her feet. "What is it, Beau? Your head? Maybe we should go back to the emergency room before we leave for Charleston." She hovered over him as he lay almost prone on the bed. Through the side of her silly little overalls he could see the curve of her breast. His hand itched to slide into that opening and explore.

She laid a cool palm across his forehead, and he closed his eyes meekly, determined to enjoy her touch as long as possible. "I'm fine," he said. "Just this infernal headache."

"Poor Beau." Her husky voice was a soft caress that slid down his spine like a low-intensity electric shock. He felt her hand move to his shoulder, and he had to peek. She tipped the last two pills from a small bottle and handed him a glass of water. "Time for these," she said with a smile that twisted his insides in a knot. "This will let you sleep in the car."

He sat upright in shock, almost knocking the glass out of her hand. "You can't drive my car."

She frowned. "I already have."

He looked at her blankly.

She lifted a shoulder. "Last night from the stadium to the hospital and from the hospital here. I was careful, I swear."

The block of time she was referring to was a complete blank. The Porsche was a powerful, masculine machine. He couldn't imagine little Kallie at the wheel.

Her brows came together, and she glared as if she could read his mind. "Don't be an ass, Beau Donovan. There's no way around it. You can't drive under the influence."

He panicked. No one, not even his dad, had driven his beautiful car. "I won't take the pills," he said rashly. "I'll be okay."

She got right up in his face. "You have a head injury," she said slowly, spacing and emphasizing the words as if he was mentally slow. "You could pass out. Your vision isn't a hundred percent. You will not drive the car. Capisce?"

He swallowed hard, momentarily distracted from thoughts of his high-performance automobile. This close he could see the little flecks of amber in Kallie's pretty, deep brown irises. Her breath was coming quickly, and her lower lip had a trace of jelly from the toast she had consumed moments ago.

He wanted to taste that jelly . . . badly.

She touched his chin. "Open your mouth, Beau."

He didn't move a muscle, not because he was being stubborn, but because he was afraid if he did he would grab her and kiss her senseless.

Apparently she took his lack of response personally. Big tears welled in her eyes, and her chin wobbled.

Oh, shit . . . crying women scared the crap out of him. He reached for her, but she batted his hands away, collapsing on the end of the bed and sobbing almost silently. Her narrow shoulders shook, and he hadn't a clue what he'd done to trigger such a deluge of tears.

He scooped her into his arms, ignoring the pain in his head. He cuddled her close, petting her and saying stupid sappy stuff he'd probably regret later.

He used the sheet to wipe her face, but the tears kept coming. "Kallie, sweetheart . . . please tell me why you're crying."

She sat up suddenly, nearly whacking his chin with her head. "I'll tell you why," she said with a hiccuping glare. "You were unconscious. I thought you might die. I had to wake you up all night long so you wouldn't go into a coma. I've had about three hours of sleep total, and now I find out you don't even trust me enough to drive your stupid, macho, look-at-my-big-penis Porsche." She was yelling by the time she got to those last six words.

He blinked in astonishment. Kallie was not a temperamental kind of woman. She was levelheaded and dependable and funny. She spaced out occasionally when she was working, but she wasn't a prima donna. She did not throw temper tantrums.

Finally he saw the past night through her eyes, and he tried for a moment to imagine what it would have been like if Kallie had been the one knocked unconscious. He'd have been scared to death. The realization humbled him. He winced as he acknowledged what a jerk he'd been. Maybe his brains were scrambled, but that was no excuse.

He picked up the glass and pried the pills from her fist.

With one long gulp of water, he swallowed them down. He cocked his head and gave her a penitent grin. "Forgive me?"

She sniffed and used the sheet for her nose. "Yes," she muttered.

He couldn't help what happened next. A wave of tenderness swamped him, and it seemed the most natural thing in the world to put his arms around her and find her mouth in a kiss of gratitude. "Thanks for taking such good care of me," he whispered. The jelly tasted sweet, but not nearly as sweet as her lips. He could make a meal off of her mouth and never go hungry again.

She returned the kiss with soft, clinging lips, and he could still feel the tremor in her body as she tried to regain her equilibrium.

He gathered her closer and slid his hands beneath the straps of her overalls, caressing her back. He held her tightly, feeling off balance and unsure of himself. This was Kallie, his buddy, his friend. He would do anything in the world to keep from hurting her. And he was in no shape to make a move right now.

Physically, maybe. His body seemed more than eager to go for the goal, despite his aching head. But even though he had thought for a long time about making love to Kallie, they were hardly in a position to be taking first steps.

She was exhausted and overwrought. He was beat-up and drugged. They might have skipped a few steps tonight in the official boy-meets-girl handbook, but that was no reason to blunder ahead without a plan.

He stroked the back of her head, winnowing his fingers through the silky curls of her ponytail. "How 'bout we get out of here?" he said, trying his best to keep his voice matter-of-fact. They were on dangerous ground, and he didn't trust himself at the moment. He wanted nothing more than to strip her out of what little she was wearing and spread her out on the bed like a feast . . . to bury his cock inside her and screw her until his energy gave out.

She sat back, sniffing again and rubbing her eyes with the heel of her hand. "Yeah, okay. If you're sure you're ready."

"Let's go home."

Kallie drove like an old lady on Sunday for the first thirty minutes. Though he tried to hide it, Beau was not entirely comfortable in the passenger seat. He did love this car.

She had to admit, the high-end Porsche was sex on wheels. Given half a chance and an open road, she could floor the accelerator and feel invincible. But she reined in her reckless impulses, determined not to give Beau a heart attack on top of his other injuries.

He finally dozed off, and although his head was bent at an uncomfortable angle, the drugs did their work, and he slept all the way home.

He lived in an upwardly mobile neighborhood of single-family homes and very nice condos. She'd been there a few times, but always in a group. Never with Beau alone.

There was a chain pharmacy down the street, so she

pulled in just long enough to get his prescription filled. He barely noticed.

He came fully awake only when she turned into his driveway and reached across his legs to get the garage door opener out of the glove compartment. She clicked it, waited a few seconds, and then eased the car inside. It was a tight fit, and she held her breath until she turned off the engine.

Beau gave her a sleepy smile. "Nice parking job."

She grinned ruefully. "Thanks."

While Beau unlocked the door to the house, Kallie gathered up her purse, his baseball glove, and the paperwork from the hospital.

Inside, the awkward level went from minimal to intense. She hated to leave him alone, but offering to stay seemed presumptuous.

Beau rescued her from a morass of indecision. "You want to hang out for awhile?" he asked, as though it was no big deal.

She nodded, feeling heat in her cheeks. "Sure. It doesn't seem like a good idea for you to be here alone while you're taking narcotics." There . . . that sounded nice and professional.

He made it as far as the den and collapsed on the couch. His face mirrored his discomfort, and her heart squeezed. "Wouldn't you be more comfortable in bed?" she asked, unable to resist the urge to brush the hair back from his forehead.

He groaned. "I'd rather stay here and have you keep me company."

"Okay." She hesitated. "You want something to drink?"

"Iced tea would be great."

She left him flipping channels and went to his kitchen. It was neat as a pin. He probably didn't eat at home very often. Fortunately, she was able to find what she needed, and in fifteen minutes she returned with a tall, icy glass.

He murmured his thanks and downed it rapidly. The bruise on the side of his head was changing color, and it looked worse than it had last night.

She perched on a chair across from him. "Do you want an ice pack for your head?"

He pulled his attention from the TV, his eyes surprisingly alert. "I'd rather have you come over here and let me put my head in your lap."

Wow. That took the wind out of her sails. She licked her lips, her throat dry. "Oh. Well, okay." Was she imagining the note of challenge in his voice?

He sat up long enough for her to get situated at one end of the big, comfy sofa, and then he lay back with a sigh.

Kallie felt frozen in place, afraid to move. She told herself she didn't want to jostle his injured head. The touch of his hair against her bare thigh was already making things happen between her legs. She would be mortified if he realized her panties were damp.

He seemed completely relaxed, and she reminded herself that he was taking happy pills. He was so mellow, surely he would never notice her sexual response.

Her hand had a mind of its own. She couldn't resist playing with his hair, stroking his forehead, trying to erase the pain lines. Beau groaned and shifted. Now his head rested against her belly.

She continued her light caress, lazily tracing the shape of his head, carefully avoiding his injury. She wanted to touch his nicely sculpted lips, but she didn't dare.

Eventually, he fell asleep again. She sat there for the longest time, thinking about his kiss in the hotel room. She wasn't going to read too much into it. He'd been grateful. That's all. And hopefully her own response hadn't been too revealing. That was a humiliation she would rather forget.

His crack about her paintbrush and his momentary nudity was harder to fathom. He'd sounded sarcastic, maybe frustrated, possibly angry. No way would she ever be able to ask again about painting him. Look what had happened the first time. Getting Beau alone in her studio in the buff just wasn't going to happen.

And even though their present situation was far more intimate than anytime they'd been together in the past, she would feel like scum if she took advantage of him now. Seducing a man with a head injury, particularly a concussion she was partly responsible for, just didn't seem fair. So she would have to bide her time, and maybe in the future she could try again before her pact with Catherine and Gina expired.

She slipped away after awhile and carefully lowered his head to the sofa. She covered him with an afghan and returned to the kitchen, this time to fix him a grilled cheese and some soup. She made enough for herself as well. Once they had finished eating, she would call a cab and make her exit.

He came ambling down the hallway when she carried the tray of food out. He had shaved and combed his hair. His eyes looked brighter, and he had some color in his cheeks.

Her knees trembled, and she gripped the tray tightly. "I made dinner, such as it is."

He sniffed. "Smells great."

They sat side by side on the sofa and ate in companionable silence. She'd made him two sandwiches to her one. He wolfed them down and finished off his soup in record time.

She insisted he rest some more while she loaded the dishwasher. When the kitchen was spotless again, she dried her hands on a towel and steeled herself for what she had to do.

She entered the den with a bright smile. "I'm going to call a cab. You've got plenty of stuff in the fridge for breakfast, and I'll call and check on you in the morning."

His face darkened to a scowl. "You're leaving?"

His clear displeasure startled her. "Well . . . I thought you'd be okay on your own now."

"What if I pass out? Have a relapse?"

She frowned. "You seem fine."

His jaw thrust forward mulishly. "Well, I'm not. But if you have more important things to do, I certainly understand."

She rolled her eyes. Beau doing the pitiful act was a sight to see. She sighed. "What exactly do you want me to do?"

He cocked his head. He was leaning against the arm of

the sofa, his legs outstretched. He linked his hands behind his neck. "Why do you want me to pose nude, Kallie?"

Shock left her gasping like a beached fish. "I . . . uh . . . well, I want to practice my oils more, and I would feel weird asking a stranger."

"And you thought I would be comfortable with this? Being naked in your studio?"

She shrugged. "I thought men were more blasé about stuff like that. I didn't think you would care."

He lifted an eyebrow. "About being nude in front of you, Kallie? Hell, yes, I'll care. But that doesn't mean I won't do it."

A lick of heat throbbed in her sex. "Oh."

His gaze was locked on her face, assessing, studying her expressions. "What happens first in that whole process?"

She shoved her hands in her pockets, fists tight, feeling her fingernails dig into her flesh. "Well, I would have to do a lot of sketches in the beginning."

"So, no paint until much later."

"Correct." She wasn't sure where he was headed.

He stood up and approached her, but she stood her ground.

He took her chin in his hand, lifting it so he could see her eyes. The disparity in their heights put her at a distinct disadvantage. "Is perfecting your art the only reason, Kallie?" His eyes were the warm blue of the Mediterranean. He wasn't smiling, but little golden lights danced in his irises, and his whole body was tensed. His fingers on her skin felt like hot brands.

The moment of truth had arrived with a shocking lack of preparation on her part. She could bail or she could step up to the plate. Beau had offered her the perfect pitch. Letting it go by would be the biggest mistake of her life. She closed her eyes and swung. "No."

Without warning, he scooped her up and carried her back to the sofa. He laid her down carefully and sat on the coffee table, just inches away. She tried to sit up, but he put a firm hand on her shoulder.

He stared at her for what seemed like an eternity. His face was completely serious, and his shoulders were rigid. "Why else would you ask me to pose nude?"

Oh, sweet heaven. She sucked in a breath, feeling lightheaded. "Because I thought it might give me an opportunity to seduce you."

His eyes went wide and blank for a half second, and his cheekbones flushed a dull red. He cleared his throat. "I see."

Her stomach began to churn. "I know we're just pals and all, and I didn't have any kind of long-term relationship in mind. But I've been wondering what it would be like to go to bed with you, and I decided . . . what the hell."

The speech was half-bravado, half-lies, but it got the message across.

He frowned. "You mean casual sex."

She summoned a smile. "Sure."

"Liar." He leaned forward, his thumb stroking her jaw. "You don't do casual sex."

Damn. She hadn't counted on the fact that he knew her

so well. She backpedaled. "Not with strangers, no. That's dangerous and stupid. But you're my friend. You're safe."

Now he looked insulted. "Listen, cupcake. No man likes to be told he's safe. That's like waving a red flag in front of a bull. Deliberately provoking the beast. Any man worth his salt would want to prove you wrong."

He laced his words with a taunting sexual challenge. And her body responded predictably. Every nerve shivered and sparked. She couldn't admit that all she had ever wanted was to be his lover. She wasn't ready to be that vulnerable, not yet. But he definitely seemed interested in her agenda, so that was a start.

She smiled placatingly. "Maybe 'safe' was the wrong word. I meant familiar."

His hand was on her collarbone now, making it difficult to breathe. His eyes were hooded. "The way I feel right now isn't familiar at all." His muttered words seemed part protest, part complaint.

He leaned forward as if in slow motion, giving her plenty of opportunity to protest. This wasn't gratitude. This was hungry intent.

When his mouth closed over hers, she whimpered. She ached from her nipples to her throbbing sex. Beau's tongue probed gently, demanding entrance. She opened to him, gasping as heat spread like wildfire.

Her arms came around his neck, and she held him close, remembering in the last second to be careful of his bruised head. But Beau seemed to have forgotten entirely about his head injury. He was kissing her like he was starving.

She knew the exact instant he realized how far out of control the kiss had gotten. He went perfectly still and backed away, his chest heaving.

His eyes glittered. "Go home. Pack a bag and get your sketch pad and pencils. And then come back. Spend the night with me."

Four

"Spend the night with me." Beau's impetuous words rang in her ears all the way home. He'd tried to get her to take the Porsche, but she hadn't needed the grand gesture, didn't want the responsibility.

The cab dropped her off, and she paid the fare hurriedly. Inside her apartment, she was all thumbs. She was nervous and excited and scared to death. Did Beau's quietly worded invitation mean what she thought it did? Did he want to have sex with her?

It had taken every bit of courage she had ever possessed to admit she wanted him. Of course, she had hedged her bets. She had omitted a few pertinent details. Like the fact that she was head over heels in love with him. That was guaranteed to make a happily single bachelor run screaming in the opposite direction.

So, she had lied. By omission. She studied her conscience for a minute. Regrets? None. Did that make her a bad person? She'd never pledged to Catherine and Gina that she would confess her undying love to the one man who had the power to break her heart. All she'd promised was to "go for it." In other words, seduce the guy who haunted her dreams and made her sweat.

That man was Beau Donovan. And tonight when he kissed her, he definitely wasn't thinking "friend" or "one of the guys." He'd been looking at her with all the hunger a man feels for a woman. And the little fillip of power and pleasure that realization gave her was pretty damned spectacular.

She felt ready to leap tall buildings in a single bound, which was quite a feat for a woman who had trouble reaching the top shelf of her closet.

She grabbed up a satchel with a couple of sketchbooks and a set of charcoal pencils. Then she threw bras and panties in a small suitcase with abandon. Some shorts, a few T-shirts, a pair of jeans, and finally—three sets of extremely naughty lingerie. She'd worn them on many occasions, but only for her own enjoyment. Victoria's Secret was one store where her petite stature didn't matter. She definitely looked grown-up in mesh and ribbons and lace. She hoped the experience would be far more interesting in Beau Donovan's bed.

She packed too much for a single night, but who knows . . . her nursing duties might be extended. It didn't hurt to be prepared.

On the way back, this time in her own car, she lectured herself. Despite that earth-shattering kiss, Beau was in no condition to play mattress games. He needed to recover, and she was determined to make sure that he rested.

As it happened, he didn't give her any arguments. By

the time she returned, he was looking much the worse for wear. When he answered the door, she exclaimed in dismay. His face was gray, and his eyes were dark with pain. She shooed him inside.

"You didn't take your medicine, did you?" she asked, dropping her things and herding him back to the couch. He sat down and slumped forward with his elbows on his knees, his head cradled in his hands. "I thought I could get by with ibuprofen."

She bit back the urge to yell at him. It wouldn't help anything, even if it made *her* feel better. She made a quick call to the pharmacy to make sure it was okay to use the prescription on top of what Beau had already taken. When she returned to the den, she found him sprawled on his back with his arm over his face.

She nudged his knee and perched on the coffee table, studying his wan face with concern. "Here's your medicine."

He groaned and rolled to a sitting position. Kallie handed him the pills and offered the glass of water in silence. She glanced at her watch. "I know it's only nine o'clock, but I think you should probably go on to bed. You needed more rest today." She was frustrated with herself for not doing a better job of looking out for him. Men were notoriously bad patients.

Beau mumbled a complaint as she pulled him to his feet, but he headed down the hall anyway. She gave him time to shower and get into bed before she brought him a cup of steaming hot tea.

He was just getting settled under the covers when she

walked into the bedroom. He turned up his nose when she handed him the cup. "Tea?"

"I keep a few bags in my purse. It's herbal decaffeinated, and it will help you sleep."

"As long as somebody doesn't wake me up all night long."

"The doctor told me to do that," she said, irritated by his grumpy obtuseness.

He gave her one of those grins that made her knees weak. Even in his rumpled condition it was lethal. "I know, munchkin. I'm just giving you a hard time. You've been an angel, and I appreciate it."

He finished the tea without complaint and handed her the cup. She turned to leave, but he grabbed her hand. "Sleep with me. Please."

Their gazes clashed, hers wary and uncertain, his for once not teasing at all. His eyelids were heavy, his jaw tight. None of his usual masculine confidence was in evidence. He looked tired and even vulnerable.

She hesitated, not sure what to say.

He tugged her closer. "I'm in no shape to assault your virtue, darlin'. Just sleep. That's all." His fingers were warm and hard against her wrist. Her pulse went haywire.

She swallowed. "All right. I'll be back in a few minutes." How could she turn him down? She would choose to be in Beau's bed under any circumstances.

She showered in record time and gazed ruefully at the flimsy sleepwear she had packed. No way was she waltzing back into that bedroom wearing any of those. She pulled out a navy baseball jersey she had thrown in at the last minute. It was a men's small, and it dwarfed her, but it covered all the important stuff.

She made sure the doors were locked and the lights turned off, and then she walked down the hall feeling like Joan of Arc headed for the stake. She might achieve sainthood herself if she managed to sleep in Beau Donovan's bed for a second unconsummated night.

All the lights were out in his room except for the small lamp on the far side of the bed. Beau's eyes were closed, his broad, hair-roughened chest bare above the sheet. One arm was flung over his head. The other lay by his side. She didn't dare speculate what he wore, or didn't wear, from the waist down. Not if she hoped to get a wink of sleep.

She quietly clicked off the light and slipped into bed with a sigh. Despite the stealth of her movements, he muttered and turned in her direction. "Kallie?" His voice was already slurred with drowsiness.

"I'm here. Go back to sleep."

She heard him move, and suddenly his big hand was at her waist, dragging her across the no-man's-land to his side of the large mattress.

It was embarrassing how little of a struggle she put up. Her body was limp and pliable as Beau tugged her closer and settled her in his embrace. "That's nice," he mumbled.

Now she knew for sure what he wore beneath the sheet. Zip. Zilch. Nada. All she could feel was hard bone and sinew and hot skin. She told herself she should protest, but she couldn't really work up any enthusiasm for that plan.

Exhaustion was catching up with her, and Beau's big warm body was wrapped around her like a comforting blanket. In seconds, he was comatose.

Her heart was fluttering in her chest, but at the moment, even feeling his nude body at her back was secondary to the fatigue dragging her under. She lay in the dark for a few minutes, savoring the pleasure of being held in his arms, and then she, too, gave up and fell asleep.

Beau awoke with a jerk, his heart pounding. He'd had crazy dreams, and it took a few seconds to orient himself. His house. He was at home. Then it all came back. The ball game. His aching head. The hospital. The hotel. And through it all, Kallie. The woman who slept so peacefully in his arms.

He craned his neck and peeked at the clock. Four a.m. He rarely slept more than seven hours a night, and now he was wide awake. He closed his eyes and studied the ache in his head. Even though the pain meds had worn off, he felt decent. Nothing worse than a dull throb.

Finally, he allowed himself to concentrate on the soft warm body curled against his. She was better than the most potent narcotic. He ran his hand down her arm, over her hip. The shirt she was wearing was bunched at her waist, and her slender legs were bare. He explored farther and encountered a miniscule pair of thong panties.

He lay there in the dark imagining what those tiny undies might look like. Red? Pink? Virginal white? He dressed and redressed her in his mind, playing a sort of blind man's fashion show.

Now that his pain was at minimal levels, his libido was firmly back in the driver's seat. He'd promised her sleep only. Would she hold him to it?

He palmed one cheek of her sweet ass and groaned. His thumb slid beneath the almost nonexistent panties and traced the sweet divide of her butt.

He shifted carefully and rolled her to her back. Now he was free to slide his hand under her shirt. Her skin was like warm satin. He traced her hip bones, the dent where he found her navel, her ribs, and, finally, her small breasts. Their contours were like Kallie herself, delicate and perfect.

She murmured in her sleep, and her nipples peaked. He rubbed them lazily, one at a time, careful not to exert too much pressure.

Then he couldn't help himself. He allowed his fingers to drift lower, retracing his steps until he ruffled the soft tuft of hair between her legs. He parted the folds guarding her secrets and found her clitoris. She was moist and warm.

His cock was so hard, he had to wince and shift to a more comfortable position. He slid one finger inside her pussy and stroked gently. Kallie sighed and lifted against his hand. His own breathing was coming faster. He was playing a dangerous game.

And he couldn't in all good conscience proceed. If they were lovers already, it might have been romantic. But not for the first time. Not like this. He whispered in her ear. "Kallie. Wake up, honey." He had to repeat his request twice.

Finally she muttered and stirred. "Beau?"

The room was almost completely dark, but he sensed the moment she came fully awake. He kissed her softly, though his body demanded more. "I want to make love to you." It came out sounding more harsh and desperate than he intended.

She was perfectly still. Only the mingled sounds of their breathing were audible.

"Are you sure?" In those three small words he heard the doubts that had plagued him for months. He didn't want to lose her as a friend.

But at the moment he was blind to other concerns. He kissed her hard, rapidly losing control of the situation. "God, yes."

She touched his cheek. "Then, let's do it, Beau. Why are we waiting?"

He turned to get a condom, but she stopped him. "I'm on the pill," she said, her voice husky.

Sweet heaven. Just thinking about being inside her, skin to skin, almost made him come. "I'm clean," he muttered.

He heard her giggle. "I know that. Can we get on with this?" She took him in her hand.

He wasn't accustomed to humor in the bedroom, but he liked it. Kallie always made him laugh, even now when he would have sworn he couldn't.

He settled between her legs and felt her flinch. "Kallie?"

She sighed. "Is this going to work?"

He understood that they were talking about physical stuff now. He was so big, and she was so small. He had a few qualms of his own. "Do you want to be on top? Would that be better?"

"No. I've fantasized about having you take me like this. I'm not giving that up."

Her bold confession notched up his arousal. By god, they would make this happen. "We'll do it," he promised rashly.

He probed at the entrance to her sex with a litany in his head. *Careful, careful, careful.* She was so small and tight, and the pressure on his cock was excruciatingly sweet. He heard her gasp. He reached between them to stroke her clit. "Relax, baby." His voice was hoarse. His arms trembled.

He eased an inch deeper. Her body tensed. He held there for a moment, giving her time to adjust. "Is it okay?"

He felt her tiny nod. She was plenty wet, but there was so much of him and so little of her. He tried again. She took a couple more inches, but he was nearing the edge. He withdrew partially and slid back in, still not completely seated in her vagina. He heard a distinct moan of pleasure, so he repeated the movement.

But his body betrayed him. With the force of a freight train, his climax bore down on him. Even in the blind surge for completion, he clung to one thought. He couldn't hurt her. He managed several more shallow thrusts, and then he pulled out and shot come all over her belly with a groan. Seconds later he rolled to his back, his chest heaving and his brain mush.

Suddenly the distance between them seemed like an

endless chasm. He felt her get out of bed, and then the bathroom light clicked on. He heard the water running. When she came back, light spilled from the door she had left ajar.

She handed him another dose of medicine. "No," he ground out, feeling ashamed and surly. The orgasm had shattered his skull in a million fragments, each one of them a sliver of pain.

"One last time," she insisted. "If you feel okay tomorrow, you can take something else. But a few more hours of solid rest won't hurt you."

He swallowed them just so she would come back to bed. When the room was dark again, she joined him and didn't protest when he pulled her close. Her feet were cold, and he tucked them between his legs.

He heard her sigh. "Good night, Beau."

He kissed her temple. "Good night, Kallie."

Sunlight was streaming into the room when he resurfaced the next time. His mouth was cottony from the narcotic, and his stomach growled. Surprisingly, his head felt a lot better.

When he sat up, the first thing he saw was the small folded note on the bedside table.

Dear Beau,

Sorry for leaving so abruptly, but I was honestly embarrassed to face you this morning. Last night was difficult on many levels, and I needed some time to think

things through. We've had an awful lot of forced together-
ness in the last forty-eight hours, and I'm guessing you
might want some time to get your head straight as well.
If you're still interested in posing for me, why don't you
plan on coming to my studio Saturday afternoon at three?
I'll do those sketches we talked about and maybe after-
wards we can go out to eat. I hope you feel much better
today. Don't forget to make an appointment for your doc-
tor to take a look at your head.

Kallie

He reread it three times, feeling his masculine confidence shrivel to pea size. It didn't take a genius to figure out
that Kallie hadn't had an orgasm last night. And they'd not
been able to manage the mechanics without hurting her.
Not to mention the fact that he had promised no sex and
then had unfairly pressured her.

All in all, a dismal disaster.

He studied the note again and couldn't find a shred of
evidence that she might like to try again. She hadn't even
signed the damned thing with any kind of hopeful saluta-
tion . . . no "love," or "fondly," or "yours."

She'd reiterated her interest in having him pose, but
that was the artist speaking. And the sexual encounter that
had rocked his world hadn't even merited a mention. Unless
you counted that veiled reference to "difficult." He winced.
Clearly being drugged and concussed had an adverse impact

on his good sense *and* his performance. He was a first-class idiot.

He'd wanted Kallie for months, and when she finally indicated an interest, he'd botched everything, maybe beyond repair.

He dressed and headed for work, regardless of his shaky legs and tender skull. If he had to stay in his house another minute, he'd go insane.

Kallie went into hiding. She e-mailed Gina and Catherine and her mother so they wouldn't call or come by. She concocted a convincing story about a rush job for a painting that was so important that she had to drop everything and couldn't be disturbed.

Then she locked all the doors and pulled down the shades and wallowed in her humiliation. Why had she ever thought she was capable of fun, lighthearted sex? She'd had her chance with Beau Donovan, and she'd blown it. She had been so nervous and uptight, he hadn't even been able to go all the way.

Every time she thought about it, she wanted to howl with misery and embarrassment. It was bad enough that she looked like a child. Now Beau had proof positive that she wasn't woman enough for him.

It had started out okay. When she woke up and felt his hands all over her skin, she had melted with longing. Every place he touched flamed into life, aching and arching and trembling with hunger.

His fingers had been so gentle, his deep, ardent kisses so drugging. She had reached for him in the dark, and that was when the trouble began. When her hand closed around his erect shaft, her heart shuddered and stopped for several beats. Beau Donovan's cock was in stunning proportion to the rest of his big body, and then some. It would never fit.

But she had tried anyway. Feeling the blunt head of his penis pushing into her made her see spots in front of her eyes. It was the most amazing feeling. Desire swept through her, hot and insistent, frightening in its power. But when he pushed against her, she had tensed, afraid that he would hurt her.

He'd been infinitely careful, but she had been unable to fully relax. In the end, he had pulled out rather than force himself on a woman who was clearly not ready for him.

She wasn't a shrinking virgin. She'd had sex before. A handful of times. But the two guys she'd dated seriously, one in college and one a few years later, had gone out with her primarily because she was one of the few women who made them feel superior. Each of them had been barely five foot seven. They loved going out with Kallie because they were actually taller than she was. Sad but true.

In each instance it had taken her far too long to figure out that her tiny stature was what made her attractive in their eyes, and each relationship had ended badly. In retrospect, the two penises that she had assumed were average were actually far below the norm in size.

Beau Donovan knocked the norm on its ass.

Was it actually possible for a man and a woman not to fit? Maybe she could talk to her doctor. Her mother would have a genteel coronary if Kallie brought up the subject. And Catherine was so shy, she would probably be just as bad. Gina would be willing to talk about it, but how exactly did one broach such a subject?

The longer she fretted about it, the more she became convinced that her wild fling with Beau Donovan was over almost before it had begun. She couldn't put herself through that agonizing uncertainty again. She had fulfilled her pact with Catherine and Gina, at least to the letter of the law. She had done what she had to do. Nothing to feel guilty about.

Saturday morning she would call Beau at work and leave him a message about an urgent prior commitment. Then she would change her name, move to the West Coast, and start a new life as a celibate little person.

She felt hysterical laughter bubbling up and couldn't stop it. She chortled and snickered and hee-hawed until the tears of laughter segued into tears of disappointment and regret.

She'd known that making a play for Beau was a long shot. But she'd never allowed herself to contemplate failure. And now she knew. There were worse things than never having sex with Beau Donovan.

Beau's mental state ran the gamut over the next few days. At first he'd been mad at Kallie for leaving. But then his anger shifted to himself. Their relationship had been increasing in intimacy. All he had to do was take things slowly. Pose for her. Flirt with her. Fool around with first date kind of stuff. Some serious necking. A few dozen hot and heavy kisses.

Even though they had known each other practically forever, they hadn't known each other in this new light. As potential lovers. And he was rapidly finding out that it was a whole different ball game.

To make things worse, he'd rushed things. And taken her by surprise. Although he'd clearly heard her say yes in the middle of the night, his nocturnal seduction had been less than fair. No wonder she was nervous. And the size issue was more of a factor than he had anticipated. Just thinking about the hot squeeze of her pussy around his cock made him break out in a sweat.

No way was he giving up on that. On them. Kallie Bradshaw was his. Period. He had been too cowardly to let her know how he felt, and thank god she had finally made the first move. She felt it, too. The connection. The heat. The attraction that had rapidly deepened into something else.

Saturday was a busy day at the restaurant, but he abandoned his staff without a qualm. They could hold down the fort without him. He had far more important business to take care of today.

He worked out at the gym for a couple of hours to take the edge off his nagging lust, and then after lunch he showered and shaved. He'd had his hair cut yesterday, and finally, he picked out a shirt that Kallie had given him for his birthday. It was a deep blue button-down. She had teased him about how it matched his eyes. In retrospect it seemed like a good sign.

It was humbling to admit how nervous he was as he

drove to her studio. Her silly little phone message hadn't fooled him one bit. He knew Kallie Bradshaw, and he knew when she was lying.

Sure enough, her car was parked by the curb. Kallie's great-aunt owned one of the famous bed-and-breakfast places down by the Battery. For an arm and a leg, tourists could enjoy being pampered and relaxed in one of Charleston's most famous locations.

The fourth-story attic had been completely renovated five years ago as Kallie's studio. He'd seen it only twice, but he'd been impressed by the airy skylights and the beautiful views of the water.

He climbed the private back stairs and knocked at the heavy wooden door. It would take dynamite to break it down, and he liked the fact that Kallie was safe even when she worked late at night.

He heard a rustle of sound inside and saw the curtain over the closest window twitch.

The door opened a crack. He stuck his toe in the opening just in case.

Half of her face appeared. "I've got a bad cold," she whispered in a ridiculously fake voice.

He grinned. "You know I never catch anything. Let me in."

"I don't feel like sketching today," she muttered, looking panicked.

"I'm surprised you're back so soon from your *prior commitment*."

The portion of her face he could see turned red. "I had to cancel that, too," she stuttered. "At the last minute."

"Because of the cold," he added helpfully.

Her one eye narrowed. "Yes."

He eased the door open and literally pushed his way in. "The jig's up, little liar. I'm here to pose for you, and I expect some great results."

Five

$\mathcal{K}$allie allowed herself to be pushed aside as Beau muscled his way into her private domain. Her first thought was almost ludicrous. *Thank god I washed my hair this morning.* Was she nuts? Clean hair was the least of her worries.

Beau wandered around her studio as if he owned the place. He examined a couple of partially finished canvases, looked out the window, and generally made himself at home. It wasn't the first time he had been here, but on the previous occasions, other people had diluted the effect.

Now it was just the two of them. Alone. In a quiet, secluded, completely private pied-à-terre. In many ways this special space felt more like home than home did. Her apartment served its function, but here, in her tucked-away Charleston garret, she thrived.

Only now she didn't feel nearly as relaxed as she usually did. Now, seeing Beau in the flesh, every yummy inch of him, she was at a loss. All she could think about was that note she had left for him and the night that preceded it.

She found herself wringing her hands, so she tucked

them in the pockets of her khaki shorts. The shirt she had on was clean, but the raspberry cotton was marred with flecks of paint.

Beau started unbuttoning his shirt. "Well, munchkin, let's get started."

She froze, watching in stunned amazement as bits of his tanned abs appeared. Surely he didn't mean what she thought he meant.

"Um, Beau . . ." She definitely wasn't up for another round of humiliation.

He lifted an eyebrow in inquiry. "The sketches, Kallie? Shouldn't we get started?" His face was perfectly serious, but his eyes danced with humor.

She let out the breath she was holding. "Oh, sure. Yeah." She waved a hand. "You can change behind that screen, and there's a robe you can put on."

He shook his head, smiling with apparent good humor as he unbuckled his belt. "I don't need a robe. You've seen it all anyway."

And in front of her shocked eyes, he stripped without ceremony. When he was buck naked, he stretched out on the less than attractive green tweed sofa. His skin was a golden bronze all over except for a strip of white around his hips.

His long legs were well shaped and lightly dusted with hair. His broad chest and strong arms were corded with just the right amount of muscle. His sex, though quiescent, hung heavy against his thigh, cushioned by his balls.

She turned away, feeling as faint as a Victorian maiden, and pretended to be busy with a small easel. She couldn't quite catch her breath. Beau was six feet away. Nude. God help her.

She reached for a professional calm, trying to remember what it was like to sketch a nude in one of her graduate classes. Nothing like this. She would have remembered this feeling. This manic mix of excitement, dread, and professional interest.

Doggedly, she forced herself to think like an artist. She could do this. She wouldn't look at Beau as a man. She would dissect him quadrant by quadrant, reducing him to a series of lines and shadows. That might work. Possibly. If she was lucky and she tried really hard.

Oops. Hard. There was a word to avoid. She attached a large sheet of rag paper to her easel and picked up a charcoal pencil. She would start with broad strokes first. The line from shoulder to hip. The shape of his head. The extension of his leg. No need to look at anything more intimate at this point.

Her hands were shaking, and she botched the sketch right off the bat. Cursing softly under her breath, she pretended to draw a bit more and then reached for another sheet of paper and tacked it over the first, as if that had been her intent all along.

This time she was more careful. She'd been correct about Beau . . . in a professional sense. The curves and planes of his hard, tough body were very pleasing to the eye. Of course, whether or not she would be willing to include a painting of him in one of her shows was debatable. Why give the competition an idea of what they were missing?

She paused for a moment and stepped aside to turn on her CD player. The haunting strains of a violin concerto filled the air. She often listened to classical music while she worked and found that it enhanced and stimulated her creativity.

She looked back at the sofa and frowned. Something wasn't quite right with Beau's pose. Her fault really. She hadn't given him any direction.

She abandoned her pencil and went to him, a frown of concentration on her face. Maybe it was the way his shoulders were tilted. She tucked a small pillow behind his back and pushed him deeper into the sofa's embrace. Now the legs looked wrong.

She lifted one of his ankles and pulled his leg straight. Then she lifted the other limb into a bent-knee position. She cocked her head and squinted her eyes. That was much better.

Beau broke out in a light sweat, despite his lack of clothing, in the attic's slight stuffiness. He wondered if he could convince her to open a window.

Her small hands touched his thigh, his ankle, his calf. Every brush of her fingers sent a lightning bolt of electricity straight to his groin. He'd maintained his relaxed pose by concentrating strictly on next week's liquor order for the bar. He'd tallied columns in his head and worked on profit projections.

The mundane task had enabled him not to embarrass himself, but with Kallie's decidedly impersonal caresses, he felt himself beginning to get aroused, despite his best efforts. He'd noticed the exact moment she lapsed from awkward lover mode to professional artist. The transformation was fascinating.

She was looking at him, but he had a feeling she wasn't seeing Beau Donovan at all. He might as well have been a bowl of plastic fruit.

He was a bit miffed, to tell the truth. Here he was, burning up from the inside out, yearning to get Kallie Bradshaw back in bed, but she was able to transcend their personal relationship and lose herself in her art. It nicked his pride.

Not that he wasn't proud of her. He was. Her talent awed and humbled him. And he sure as hell wanted to be her only nude model. At least on the male side of the coin. But how could she ignore what was happening between them? How could she forget making love to him, even in the short-term?

That night was indelibly imprinted on his brain. Okay, so maybe there were parts of it he would just as soon forget. Portions that made him seem pretty selfish. Possibly he would prefer an edited version. But he didn't have that choice. He couldn't forget. Even for a moment. He'd had Kallie in his bed, and it was an experience he was determined to repeat. Soon.

He tried to take a deep breath without moving. This modeling crap was hard. Already his muscles ached. And he wasn't all that good at remaining motionless for indefinite periods. Kallie had snapped at him twice, telling him to be still.

He wanted to move. Inside her. Deeper and deeper until he pressed against her womb. He closed his eyes and tried shallow breathing, feeling the hot rush of desire overtake him. His thighs quivered, imagining what it would feel like to spread hers and slide into her wet, slick heat.

He groaned and shivered.

"Beau."

Her peremptory tone snapped him back to reality.

She was frowning, her gaze directed just below his waist. "Can you please deflate that . . ."

"Erection?" he added helpfully.

She nodded slowly, her eyes still fixed on his penis. "Yes," she said, and he was pleased to hear the hoarse croak. Maybe not so professional after all.

He shrugged, trying to appear suitably penitent. "I can't help it, darlin'. Being naked with you gives me ideas."

She was turning red now. Her slender feet were bare, and she shifted back and forth, rubbing the sole of one foot against the opposite shin. "I can't draw you like that."

He kept his pose with difficulty. "Ignore it. Draw everything else. But I gotta tell you, munchkin, I doubt I'll ever be able to pose for you without this happening. You might have to sketch that last part while I'm asleep. But come to think of it, even then I'd probably be dreaming about you."

She definitely looked rattled now. Her eyes were huge, and her skin looked like she had a sunburn. She gave him furtive glances and focused her eyes on her sketch. If he hadn't been so achingly aroused, it might even have been funny.

Beau gritted his teeth and inhaled, then exhaled slowly. Damn, how long did it take to complete a simple preliminary sketch? His cock was as big and as hard as it had ever been in his memory. His skin tingled, and his heart was thumping in big, heavy jerks.

He wanted Kallie Bradshaw. Had wanted her for years, and he wasn't willing to wait much longer. Finally, she laid down her pencil and stepped around the easel.

She looked in his direction, but not quite *at* him. "I'm done. You can get dressed now. I'll step outside a minute and give you some privacy."

She was all the way to the door before he caught her. He snatched her up in his arms and lifted her against the wall until their faces were even. "Look at me," he growled, feeling the frantic beat of her heart echoing his own tumultuous pulse.

Her jaw trembled, and he felt like a heel. Maybe he'd misread the signals. Maybe she didn't want him after all. He cleared his throat. "Why are you shaking?" he asked gruffly.

Her eyelids lowered, shielding her thoughts from him. "I think we made a mistake," she whispered. "You're one of my best friends. I don't want to lose you."

A tearing pain ripped through his chest, making him light-headed. "Don't say that," he muttered. "I'll fix whatever it is."

A tear dripped off the end of her nose. "I want to go back to the way things were."

"We can't," he groaned, feeling her bare legs against his hips. His cock rubbed against her shorts. "Something changed for us, Kallie. You see that, don't you? Please tell me you do."

He carried her to the sofa and cradled her in his arms. "Don't shut me out, honey. Talk to me."

She was stiff in his embrace. Her silky curls brushed his shoulder. "Can you at least put some clothes on?" She was trying to be humorous, but she didn't quite pull it off.

He kissed her cheek. "No. I like being naked with you. I'd like it more if you'd join me, but I can be patient."

She was silent for so long, he knew he'd have to keep the conversation going or die trying. He'd planned to ease into this confession later, but now seemed like a good time. "I paid the guys to stay in Charleston and not go to the ball game with us."

That brought her head up. "Why?" Her face was streaked with tears, and the hurt in her pretty brown eyes raked him with guilt.

He stood at the edge of a mighty scary drop. He could lose her forever. "I'm in love with you, Kallie," he said simply. "I want a future with you."

Now her face went white, only a hectic spot of color on each cheekbone. She sprang away from him, and he let her go. "You can't possibly want that, Beau Donovan," she cried, looking like he had suggested something horrific. "We haven't even had sex."

That hurt. He absorbed the blow but kept his smile. "Well, one of us did."

She clenched her fists at her sides, her chest heaving. "It won't work, Beau."

He felt his dreams shatter at his feet, and his blood numbed to an icy stream in his veins. He swallowed against the boulder-sized lump in his throat. Suddenly he wished he had gotten dressed after all. He no longer felt nude and aroused. Now he felt naked and foolish. "I thought you felt something for me," he mumbled, prepared to beg. "I guess I was wrong."

She came close enough to slug his shoulder. "Of course I care for you," she yelled. "But in case you didn't notice, we weren't exactly great in bed. And it's my fault."

He went still, processing her anguished cry. He grabbed her hips, forcing her to stop pacing. "What the hell are you talking about? Of course it's not your fault." In the back of his mind, he recognized the fact that he had confessed his love, and she had not reciprocated. He'd worry about that later.

She grabbed his arms, trying to free herself. "We . . . didn't . . . fit." The raw misery and vulnerability on her face put an ache in his throat.

He dropped to his knees, nuzzling her belly with his face, hating the layer of cloth that prevented him from feeling her bare skin. But if he released her, she would bolt. "We experienced a few glitches, cupcake. That's all. The next time will be better, I promise." He spoke softly, trying to calm her frantic protests.

He felt her hands in his hair. "How is your head?" she

asked quietly. She was no longer fighting him, at least not physically. And he could hear the concern in her voice.

He inhaled her familiar perfume. "Almost good as new." His thumbs rucked up her top enough for him to be able to tongue her navel. He chuckled roughly when she moaned. "Admit it, Kallie. All evidence to the contrary, we're good together." His hands moved from her hips to her rib cage.

Two more inches and he was able to cup her breasts. He felt the tension in her body when he touched her nipples, and his hands fell away. Maybe he was wrong. He felt sick to his stomach, and he released her. "I'm sorry," he said, realizing that his formal tone was in absurd counterpoint to his lack of clothing. "I apologize if I'm making incorrect assumptions."

He got to his feet and stepped past her, reaching for his pants and pulling them on without his boxers. He felt raw and exposed, and he needed a shield between his chaotic emotions and her continuing silence.

He raked his hands through his hair. "Good lord, Kallie. You can't even stand for me to touch you anymore. Is that it?"

He finally managed to look at her. She might seem small and defenseless, but she held his future in her hands. And he wasn't accustomed to anyone having that much power over his happiness. Irritation masked his despair momentarily. "You might as well give it to me straight. Tell me the truth."

Her jaw stuck out mulishly. "I'm flat-chested."

Of all the things she might have said to him, that was

one statement he definitely hadn't prepared for. "I beg your pardon?"

Her chin lifted with heart-wrenching dignity. "I have no breasts."

He laughed. "I believe I'm the best judge of that. And you're wrong. I spent quite a bit of time the other night getting up close and personal with your pretty little tits."

Her eyes flashed. "See what I mean?" She threw out her hands. "Little."

He grinned, beginning to understand part of the problem. "They're small and perfect, Kallie. Just like you."

Some of the doubt and insecurity faded from her face, and he breathed an inward sigh of relief. But he wasn't out of the woods yet. He braced himself and ripped off the Band-Aid. "Do you love me, Kallie?"

Fresh tears welled in her eyes, but she blinked them away. "It doesn't matter."

He frowned. "It matters a hell of a lot to me. Do . . . you . . . love me?"

He wanted to hold her, but he didn't trust his control, which was unraveling. He wouldn't touch her again without the truth.

She sighed. "Of course I love you. I can't believe you haven't noticed before now."

The bottom dropped out of his stomach, but in a good way. "You might have mentioned it sooner."

She huffed. "I'm not your type."

He took a step closer. "You're exactly my type."

She shook her head frantically. "No. You've always treated me like one of the guys."

"That was so I wouldn't be tempted to rip off all your clothes and ravish you."

A tiny smile found its way onto her lips. "Did you really pay the guys?"

He nodded. "A hundred bucks apiece."

She chuckled. "That must have hurt. They'll razz you forever."

He sobered. "I would have mortgaged my business if I had to. I can't lose you, Kallie."

She nibbled her bottom lip. "You can't have a marriage without sex."

He took her shoulders in a light grip. "I don't plan to." He was talking to the top of her head, and her stubbornness frustrated him. He scooped her up and plopped her down on a large worktable, shoving supplies willy-nilly out of the way. Now he could see her face. "Sex is not going to be a problem."

Her eyes were big and dark and stormy. "How can you be so sure?"

He kissed the tip of her nose. "Because we'll just keep doing it over and over until we get it right."

Her eyes glazed over, and her breathing grew ragged. "I don't know if I can take you."

He kissed the side of her neck. "You will . . . sooner or later. It doesn't matter if it takes some time. But even if we never manage it, sex with you will still be the best I've ever had."

She pouted. "Liar. You're just saying that to make me feel better."

He chuckled. "Men aren't that altruistic, believe me. You make my head spin, Kallie darlin'." He swept her shirt off over her head and sucked in a breath. He liked this no-bra thing. She was perfect and precious. He hadn't been lying about that.

He took one bubble-gum-pink nipple into his mouth and sucked gently, then teased the other one with his fingers. Kallie moaned and shifted restlessly. He helped her to her knees so that their mouths met. She opened up to him like a flower in the sun.

He parted her lips with his tongue and thrust into the warm, sweet taste of her mouth. Already he recognized her flavor. Already he knew the shape and texture of her tongue.

He pushed her back on the table and bent over her. He lifted her hips and stripped off her shorts and panties. It was the first time he had seen her in full daylight, and it made his knees weak. He found her clit and licked it lazily.

. Kallie shuddered and groaned. He increased the pressure with his tongue, stroking against her most sensitive spot with regular movements. He murmured to her, urging her on, whispering his love.

She cried out, and he sucked gently the entire time, staying with her as she rode through the crest of bliss and slid down the other side.

She blinked at him sleepily. "I want to eat your cock."

Now there was an offer no sane man would refuse. He

scooped her up and returned to the sofa. He sprawled on his back, and she knelt between his legs. Her hair brushed his stomach as she went down on him.

Everything in his body tensed when he felt the hot suction of her tongue on his prick. Sweet Jesus. His fists clenched at his sides, and he fought the urge to howl like a wild animal baying at the moon. Pleasure was too mild a word for what he was experiencing.

He was so damned close when she stopped. She disappeared for a brief moment and returned carrying an unmarked verdigris glass bottle.

She answered the unspoken question in his eyes. "It's a special herbal oil I use to keep my hands from getting dried out."

While he watched in hungry fascination, she poured a little bit in her hand and reached between her thighs to massage herself. He bit out a curse. She ignored him. Moments later she poured more oil and gently rubbed it into his rock-hard erection.

The fluttery sensation of her fingers on his dick brought him close to the edge again. But she didn't keep up her unwitting torture for very long. She capped the bottle and set it aside.

Then she straddled his waist and moved her body into position.

He gripped her ass. "We've got nothing to prove here," he said hoarsely. "How we make love is no one's business but our own."

Her eyes were shadowed. She took his shaft into her hand and guided it to her entrance.

"Wait." He grabbed her shoulders. "Tell me we're a couple. No matter what."

She rubbed the head of his penis against her wet folds, moaning and writhing. Her murmur was indistinct. Inarticulate.

He was horny, but desperate. He couldn't take a chance. "Kallie." He said it loudly and firmly.

She blinked at him, clearly ready for the final act. "Hmmm?"

"I want a commitment."

She tried to join their bodies, but he held her off. "Say it."

She nodded, her eyes fluttering closed. "Yes. Sure. Fine. Can I screw you now?" If he hadn't been stretched on a rack of acute anticipation, with sure ecstasy hovering just off-stage, he might have managed a laugh.

He held perfectly still, allowing her to make all the moves. This had to work. He didn't want anything to come between them. "You're in charge, munchkin. Go for it. I'm right with you."

Kallie concentrated on the feel of Beau's body. She wouldn't second-guess this. Not now. Beau loved her. She chanted it inside her head as she lowered herself onto his thick, broad penis.

She wasn't prepared, despite their earlier encounter. He felt like hot steel covered in warm, supple satin. The sensation of being stretched made her breathless. She wasn't nervous this time, not really. But she wanted badly for this to work.

She eased down on his prick like a pole dancer in slow motion. His eyes were closed, and his mouth was tight in what might be called a grimace. She looked away, refusing to let her fears dissuade her.

She gained a couple more inches and had to stop for a moment. The insistent thrust of him inside her tight sheath was just this side of uncomfortable. Even though he wasn't moving. Even though he was letting her set the pace.

But she needed to feel their connection. "Beau? Are you okay?"

He opened his eyes and choked out a laugh. "Isn't that my line?" She slid down a tiny bit more, and his eyes crossed. She took his groan as a good sign.

She rocked back and forth and managed another inch. "I need you to look at me," she whispered.

He opened his eyes. "I'm not sure that's a good idea," he rasped, his jaw tight.

"Why not?"

He flexed his hips and gained more ground. "Because when I look at you like this I nearly lose my mind." The intense look in his eyes made her even hotter.

She leaned forward, changing the angle slightly. "You do the rest," she muttered. Her hands rested on his chest. "I'm okay."

She saw the indecision that skated across his face. She squeezed her inner muscles and couldn't decide whether to laugh or cry when he cursed raggedly.

He caressed her butt. "Are you sure?"

She nodded wordlessly. "Take me all the way."

He lifted her in his big hands and pulled her back down. She gasped. In this slightly new position her clitoris got the attention it craved.

Beau surged upward, possessing her almost completely. She concentrated on relaxing her muscles, crying out inwardly as he tried again. She felt a burning, pressing, riotous sensation as he lodged his flesh deeply inside hers, mating them to the final degree.

His chest was heaving, his forehead beaded with perspiration. The muscles in his arms stood out in tense cords.

She bit his nipple and he jerked, flexing his mighty hips. "Oh, god, Beau."

He touched her clit with his thumb. "Good?" he asked in a gasped question.

She nodded, incoherent with pleasure. "Yes," she whispered. "Oh, yes."

He shouted then and surged all the way in, buffeting her with a tide of hunger that triggered her climax and sent her tumbling into the abyss.

She heard him groan from deep inside his chest and felt his thigh muscles bunch and flex as he exploded in what seemed like an endless orgasm.

And afterward, he held her so close to his heart she could hear the very life force in him pumping furiously and then eventually settling into a satiated sleep.

An indeterminate amount of time later, Beau realized two things simultaneously. Kallie's bare body was entwined with his, resting on top like an erotic little kitten, and his nuts and his feet were cold. He reached for a blanket, and only then did he realize where he was. He brushed her hair from her face. "Kallie."

She mumbled and squirmed, endangering their future procreational success.

He winced. "Wake up, munchkin."

She complied, blushing adorably when she took stock of their naked abandon.

For once, his Kallie seemed speechless. He popped her on the butt. "Get dressed, my love. You promised me dinner."

She pouted and moved her lower abdomen sinuously against his. "Are you sure you're hungry?"

He managed a grin, despite the furor ensuing below his waist. "We have some shopping to do for a ring, and I have to call the radio station in Savannah and brag about the catch I made at the game."

She looked confused. "The ball hit you on the head, Beau. You never even got your glove on."

He pulled her down for a long thorough kiss, deciding that dinner could wait for a bit. "I wasn't talking about the baseball, sweetheart. I was talking about you."

Party Girl

One

Gina McCutcheon pondered the wasteland that was her sex life as she strolled the decks of the *Caribbean Princess*. The sun was shining, the sky was blue, and considering that it was the middle of January, she gave the pleasant breeze and balmy warmth two thumbs up.

Now if she could free her mind and simply vegetate for the next five days and four nights, she might be able to enjoy herself.

Catherine and Kallie were partly to blame for her somewhat stressed attitude. On two counts. They'd badgered her into this cruise thing, despite her fear of water and her tendency to burn to a crisp while sunbathing. Her only hope of ever being a sun worshipper was if some kick-ass researcher came out with an SPF Infinity. Then and only then Gina might be able to expose her Celtic-bred skin to the sun.

But the way things stood now, she was destined to spend the bulk of the cruise tucked in a shady corner, enjoying a good book, and trying not to look out at the endless ocean that might swallow her whole given half a chance. She shuddered, trying not to let images of *Titanic* make her crazy. There were no icebergs in the Caribbean or the Gulf of Mexico.

But none of her mental pep talks gave her much comfort. Now she was back to her two so-called best friends. Nine months ago they had all met to celebrate their twenty-ninth birthdays. They'd made a pact to act on a fantasy in the next year, to jump-start their sex lives, to find romance and embrace it.

She snorted cynically. Romance was for the birds. Not that she begrudged Catherine and Kallie their almost nauseating happiness. Both women had shown guts and fortitude and had sought out the men of their dreams and culled them from the pack of single, commitment-phobic bachelors who prowled the streets of Charleston looking for fresh blood.

Whoa, Gina. A little melodramatic. And more than a little bitter. She winced inwardly. Jealousy was a bitch. The truth was, neither Phillip nor Beau had put up too much of a fight. They were head over heels in love with her two best friends, and the happy couples were actually planning a double wedding for June.

Gag me with a spoon. The whole thing gave her hives. White lace. Promises. Adoring heated glances. Soft sighs in the dark. Maybe it worked for Catherine and Kallie, but Gina was made of tougher stuff. Her mother was on her third marriage, her father on his fifth. That was enough to make their only child gun-shy when it came to the topic of tying the knot.

Play with Me

There was no such thing as permanence. At least not in the McCutcheon gene pool. All those redheaded, fiery ancestors were hard-drinking, hard-living, foulmouthed fishermen. Even her mom's genteel Georgia upbringing hadn't exerted a noticeable influence. If anything, she'd been drawn over to the dark side.

Gina sighed, leaning her forearms on the rail and bravely looking out toward the horizon. At least Catherine and Kallie had a particular man in mind when they made the pact. Gina was fresh out of prospects, romantic or otherwise. She slammed the door on the painful memory that threatened to surface. That one little episode was years ago and no longer relevant.

If there had ever been a time when she was a bit softer around the edges, it was long past. Hell, even her job reinforced the message. She'd been deeply involved in Charleston's charity work for the last six years, and some of the stories she had seen and heard would rip your heart out.

Women with life-threatening diseases, five kids, and no husbands. Women with battered faces and shredded self-esteem. Families whose hollow eyes and hopeless faces spoke of the raw deal fate had dished out to them. And then there were the children. Abandoned. Mistreated. Angry and aggressive to cover their terrible insecurities. So much pain and so few advocates.

So Gina became their champion. She had the money, the influence, and the time. And with no significant other in her personal life to demand her attention, she was able to throw herself wholeheartedly into her work.

Catherine and Kallie disapproved. Not of the work, of course, but of Gina's single-minded focus. They lectured her with words like "burnout" and "balance" and "mental health." And they were the ones who insisted she needed a vacation. Gina knew in her heart of hearts that they were right, but she hated slowing down for any reason.

Because if she did, there was too much time to think. Too much opportunity to examine how she had messed up her life. Too much pain in remembering.

She looked down at the water far below and shivered. The depth and vastness of the deep turquoise sea mocked her tiny, unimportant existence. She could work tirelessly from now until she died, and any good she might accomplish would be nothing but a drop in the endless ocean of human need.

Sometimes the sheer enormity of what she tried to accomplish weighed her down. She wanted the same things most women wanted. A loving husband. Healthy children. A fulfilling career. One out of three wasn't bad, and frankly, she probably didn't deserve the rest.

She was blunt and sarcastic and had little patience with fools and sycophants. She had a temper, and she could be rude on occasion if stupid people got on her nerves. She didn't have Catherine's class. She didn't have Kallie's talent.

So it was really no surprise that she hadn't been in bed with a man in more than two years. She regarded the whole tiresome dating scene as pretentious and silly, and although she loved sex as much as the next woman, she was no longer willing to put up with all the crap that preceded it.

So, given the alternatives, she was celibate and single and happy to be so.

Liar. Her subconscious was even more rude than she was. Okay, so maybe she ached to be held in strong arms and kissed senseless. What of it? Wasn't that the point of this cruise? To get laid?

Unfortunately, someone should have researched the demographics of the passenger list before she boarded the boat. So far, her shipboard companions seemed to fall into two categories, stoop-shouldered blue hairs and scrawny octogenarians wearing plaid golf pants. All of whom were pleasant and cheerful and full of life, but their stellar qualities had little bearing on her problem.

The staff presented a few more interesting possibilities. The ship's registry was Italian, and a number of lovely men with flashing dark eyes populated the hallways. But it was clear that company policy forbade intermingling with guests on a personal level, so Gina was pretty much screwed.

Or not. That was the crux of the matter.

She sought out a comfortable lounge chair in a pocket of shade and rummaged in her tote for the latest espionage bestseller. Catching up on her reading was a worthy goal, at least in the absence of more carnal pursuits. She'd just have to tell Catherine and Gina that the pool of prospective one-night stands had been empty.

The book held her interest for a little more than an hour. That was pretty good for her. She'd been diagnosed with ADHD in high school, and she'd worked hard to improve her concentration and attention span.

But now what? It was still two hours until the first seating of dinner, and the sun was at its worst, so swimming was out. Maybe a nap. It didn't sound all that appealing. Her energy level rarely waned, and she would far rather be busy. She'd only been on board since eight o'clock that morning, and already she was restless.

Suddenly, a shadow fell over her legs. "Gina? Gina, is that you?"

The familiar voice from her past made her skin go icy and her blood freeze. Oh, no. God couldn't be that cruel. She shaded her eyes against the sun and looked up. Way up. There he stood. Trey Lipman. Thomas Lipman the Third. Financial genius. Heir to the family banking empire. Her personal nemesis. And the last man in the world she expected or hoped to see on this damned boat.

No matter how hard she tried, she couldn't manufacture a social smile. "Hello, Trey."

Trey shoved his hands in his pockets and absorbed the unspoken message in those two terse words with a heavy heart. Gina had not forgiven him.

Not that there was any reason to believe she would. He'd been a monumental jerk six years ago, and he deserved her hostility. But some small part of him had been hoping time would heal the wound.

Despite her body language, he sat on the lounge chair nearest hers, managing not to react when his knee brushed her bare leg. God, she was gorgeous. Even more beautiful than she had been at twenty-three. And that was saying something.

He felt a funny little pain in his chest. Her wavy auburn hair was pulled back in a ponytail at the moment, but he had vivid memories of how it looked tumbling around her shoulders. Her lush, beautiful breasts spilled from the top of her lavender bikini, and the rest of her body was equally curvaceous.

Her emerald eyes were hidden at the moment by aviator sunglasses, but he knew them intimately. As well as he knew the naturally sexy curve of her lips and the cute tilt of her nose.

The Lipman and McCutcheon families went way back, both in business relationships and social contexts. He'd known Gina since she was a precocious child, and he'd watched her grow up. At twenty-three she'd been living life on the edge.

He'd worried about the frantic pace, the drinking, the dieting. She'd been a lost child trapped inside a woman's body. Her parents' sexual antics and multiple marriages had confused a disturbed teenager, and she had started a pattern of acting out. By the time she graduated from college, the wild partying and lavish spending had become Gina's trademarks.

Trey was a decade older than she was, and his heart had ached for her. But his concern was more than impersonal or altruistic. In fact, he'd spent far too much time fantasizing what it would be like to be the man in her life. He'd watched her with a procession of fresh-faced, hard-bodied boys, but he doubted whether she was as promiscuous as the evidence suggested.

Gina kept people at a distance. She was extremely guarded with her real emotions, and he was pretty sure the parade of hot guys at her side was meant to play a part in the face she showed the world. A few probably shared her bed from time to time, but he'd bet his last dollar that her lovers were few and far between.

He shook his head figuratively, throwing off the memories that still pained him. Gina's eyes were on her book. His brief retreat into the past had given her time to shut him out.

He sat back in his chair and stretched out his legs. Suddenly this cruise was looking a lot more interesting than it had that morning when he'd reluctantly boarded and settled into a nicely appointed stateroom. He had plenty of patience, and he knew that Gina did not. Predictably, after only five minutes, she snapped her book shut and glared at him.

He kept his eyes fixed on the horizon, feigning relaxation. In his peripheral vision he saw her remove her sunglasses and toss them in a bag. He turned his head, taking careful note of the irritation in her clear green eyes.

He smiled blandly. "Beautiful view, isn't it?"

A frown creased her high forehead. "Why are you on this boat, Trey? I thought vacation was a dirty word in your vocabulary."

She wasn't even bothering to disguise her animosity. Her words fairly crackled with heat. He took that as a good sign. Anger was a strong emotion. Perhaps she hadn't forgiven him, but at least she wasn't indifferent.

He studied the sensual curve of her lips. Six years ago he'd been an idiot. But not anymore. He was coasting down the hill toward his fortieth birthday, and for once in his life, he wasn't going to let work get in the way of what he wanted. Never again.

He shrugged. "My grandmother gave me the cruise for a Christmas present. She thinks I'm a workaholic. A confirmed bachelor. A man with no soul."

Gina snorted. "Smart lady."

He chuckled, enjoying her sharp wit. "I love her too much to disappointment her, so here I am."

She narrowed her eyes, studying his face like she yearned to see it on a "wanted" flyer at the post office. "Did you bring your laptop?"

He felt his ears turn red. "Yes."

Her supercilious smile said she knew everything about him and didn't like what she saw. "No big surprise there. I'd say you haven't changed a bit."

He saw his opening and went for it. "But you have, Gina. I'm so proud of the woman you've become."

His quiet, sincere praise clearly stopped her in her tracks. A succession of emotions flashed through her eyes. Shock. Embarrassment. Vulnerability. But then a wall slammed down and her expression became as remote and unreadable as the opaque ocean. "We all have to grow up sometime," she said, her voice cool.

"It's more than that," he insisted. "I've been following

your career. You've done so much for so many in Charleston. It humbles me."

Now she looked distinctly uneasy. She leapt to her feet, almost tripping in the folds of her beach towel. She stuffed things in her bag with clumsy haste. "I have to go. I forgot a phone call I need to make." And just like that, she was gone.

He rubbed his hands over his face, battling disappointment and regret. After his last ugly encounter with the younger Gina, he had tried on a half-dozen occasions to apologize. But she'd been vehement in her outrage and hurt.

Not that she'd worn her heart on her sleeve. Not Gina. She'd sailed ahead with that damned chip on her shoulder, pretending to him and the world that everything was fine. But he knew he had hurt her deeply, and it had never been his intent.

He'd let his own feelings get in the way of caring for her fragile psyche, and he'd been an arrogant, pompous ass in the process. He never imagined he'd have another chance, but they were essentially trapped on this ship for another four days and nights, and he was determined to make the most of this opportunity.

It was too much to hope she'd ever look at him as anything but an annoyance. He still hadn't managed that apology, but at least he'd let her know how he felt about the life she had created for herself. Gina McCutcheon was a giver and a caretaker. She'd poured her heart and soul into her work with amazing results.

Every charitable board and foundation in the city wanted

her. She had enthusiasm and passion and drive and a dedication to those less fortunate.

Perhaps it had taken a bit of time for her to find her niche. And maybe her parents were partly to blame. But she had matured into a smart, generous, focused woman. And he hadn't been lying when he said how proud he was of her. She could have taken her daddy's money and become a Paris Hilton type.

But Gina had grit and courage, and no one could ever fault her new priorities.

Now, if the fates smiled on him, he had a shot at making up for the past. He'd like to think it could be more than that, but his feelings didn't matter. He owed Gina an apology and some groveling.

Gina made it back to her cabin on shaky legs. She slammed the door and locked it, then flopped across the bed and groaned. Of all the gin joints in the world, why did he have to walk into hers?

She could understand Ingrid Bergman's fascination with the brooding Rick. Trey Lipman had captured Gina's heart years ago, and even his contempt for her morals and her character had not been enough to extinguish that flame.

She'd thrown herself at him on one memorable occasion and been burned in the process. He was an older man, sophisticated, successful, admired by one and all. And she had been nothing but a silly, shallow princess craving attention and love.

But she'd found out the hard way that love could not be demanded from others. You had to earn it. Her parents had loved her, of course, but they were both basically narcissists. Once she hit sixteen, they gave her a sports car and her own Visa card and had basically assumed she could do the rest on her own.

There had been no whispered heart-to-hearts with her mother about sex and boys. No pat on the back from her father for good grades. Of course, in all fairness to him, the good grades had been few and far between.

She'd skated though college on her looks and the large annual gifts her parents made to her institution of higher learning. Even a professor or two had been willing to barter GPAs for sex. She'd turned them down. Yuck. Even she had some standards. But she had learned one lesson well. Money, beauty, and influence opened just about any door. Except for the one to Trey Lipman's heart.

But he'd done her a favor, really. His harsh criticism of her life and the track it was on had been a wake-up call. Desperately hurt and humiliated, she had suddenly seen herself through his eyes. And it hadn't been pretty.

Little by little she had drawn back from the edge of a world that threatened to drag her under. Her parents hadn't understood her about-face. Her party buddies had been first puzzled and then disgusted.

Only Catherine and Kallie had supported her unconditionally in her fledgling efforts at turning her life around. Even the places she had tried to volunteer were skeptical at first. She'd been a society page darling, a vibrant butterfly in the world of glitz and glamour. It had taken months for anyone to take her seriously.

But she had paid her dues both literally and figuratively. She had slowly carved a meaningful place for herself in the world of philanthropy. And it had felt good. She had worked harder and harder, determined to erase the image of herself as a flighty, self-centered, immature rich girl.

People took her seriously now.

She should be satisfied.

But today, sitting in a deck chair beside Trey Lipman, she realized that for six years she had been trying to win the approval of a man who broke her heart. Hearing him speak so eloquently about her work had stunned her. At first she had searched his words for sarcasm. For criticism. It had been a knee-jerk reaction.

But his gentle, heartfelt admiration was for real, and when she realized that, she fled. She knew well how to handle naysayers and detractors. Chin up and to hell with the world.

Compliments and praise were another story. Especially from Trey.

She'd been so shocked to see him, she had barely been able to appreciate how wonderful he looked. His whiskey brown eyes and crooked grin were as appealing as ever. A tiny bit of silver at his temples did nothing to detract from the appeal of his sun-streaked chestnut hair. He was a man confident in his own skin, always had been.

Trey had come from the same privileged, moneyed background as Gina. But unlike her, he had worked his butt

off to prove he was worthy of his place in the family business. While Gina partied and played, Trey had been putting
in long hours at the bank, building a name for himself and
earning the respect of his peers.

Trey was solid and dependable, and though those two
traits might sound boring, he was anything but. He was
sexy and charming, and young Gina had fallen hard for the
man who had often been on the fringes of her life. Neither
her contemporary nor her father's in age, he fell somewhere
in the middle.

And his steady, reassuring presence made her heart
threaten to leap out of her chest when he was close to her.
Unfortunately, he wasn't much of a social animal. It had
been a welcome surprise when he showed up one evening
at a summer garden party hosted by mutual friends.

Gina had downed three mai tais by the time he arrived.
The alcohol had done little to dull the misery and loneliness
she was battling. Trey was like a rock in the middle of a
frightening sea of uncertainty.

She had cornered him in a quiet, shadowed bit of the
yard and tried to flirt. She knew she was attractive to men.
In some nebulous, yearning place deep in her heart, she
needed to feel Trey's warmth and desire.

At first she thought she would succeed. When she
kissed him audaciously, he had responded. And oh, what a
kiss it had been. Nothing at all like the groping, clumsy kisses
of the young men she allowed close enough to try. Trey's
mouth and hands had been warm and steady and sure. No
hesitation. No fumbling.

His tongue had entered her mouth, and her knees had buckled. It had been the most exciting moment of her life to date. She'd wrapped herself around his strong body, struggling to get closer. She craved his heat, his touch, his ardor.

His erection had pressed against her, and she wanted to weep with joy. He felt it, too. Her heart had soared in her chest, and for a brief moment in time, she knew that everything wrong in her life could be fixed if this one incredible man claimed her as his own.

But the fairy tale had ended abruptly and painfully. Trey had shoved her away, his face a mask of disgust. And then he had proceeded to enumerate all of her failings in careful detail. When he was done, she had wanted to crawl in a hole and die.

Because not only was his scathing assessment extremely painful and humiliating . . . what hurt the most was that every word out of his mouth was true.

Two

Trey chatted with his dinner companions, but his attention was on the far side of the room at the captain's table. The distinguished older man in the crisp white jacket entertained a different handful of guests each evening, and he was no fool.

He'd wasted little time in snagging the most beautiful and interesting woman on the ship for his first dinner out. Even at a distance, Gina glowed. Not only her fiery auburn hair, but her. Her essence. Her warm charismatic beauty. Already her tablemates were laughing and smiling as though they had known her and one another for years.

Gina had that gift. She cared about people, and they naturally gravitated to her charm and vitality. She was the life of the party, and her inner fire brought energy and excitement to those around her.

He took a bite of his chicken marsala and sneaked another look. He didn't want to be rude to his own dinner companions, but he was compelled to follow Gina's every move. She was dressed formally in a black jersey gown that was actually quite plain.

But the halter top hugged her amazing curves, and before she had been seated, he'd seen the way the fabric clung to her sexy hips. A side slit exposed one long, shapely leg. With a body like that, the dress was merely a foil.

Diamond drop earrings dangled from her ears, and with her hair upswept in a complicated swirl, her bare neck and shoulders appeared almost demure and innocent. Until you took a glance at her bounteous cleavage. Gina looked like every man's dream. Good enough to eat. And he meant that more than metaphorically.

He kept tabs on her for the entire hour-and-a-half meal. When he saw her stand, he excused himself and followed her. He'd already noted the location of her room, but she didn't head in that direction. Instead, she wandered up to one of the topmost decks, deserted at this hour.

He kept to the shadows, watching as she leaned forward on the rail and stared out to sea. The sky above them was inky black, spattered with a million stars. The wind was light and cool.

He approached her quietly, saying her name so she wouldn't be startled.

When she heard him, she lifted her head and turned around. "Trey."

Try as he might, he couldn't read her inflection. He stood beside her, their hips almost touching. "You look beautiful tonight, Gina."

Her serene, lovely face was expressionless. "Thank you."

He sighed inwardly. She would not make this easy, he was sure of that. He exhaled. "I need to tell you something."

She shrugged one slender, bare shoulder. "It's a free country." She couldn't have made her disinterest any more clear.

He gritted his teeth and forced himself to ignore her antagonism. "I—I want to apologize for all those things I said to you six years ago."

Her chin lifted a half inch, her posture regal and cool with unspoken disdain. For him. For his fumbling words. "They were all true."

Her flat, low-voiced statement held a world of pain and regret.

He touched her forearm. "They weren't the whole truth, Gina." He saw the brief wobble of her chin before she controlled it, and he felt lower than dirt.

He wanted to hold her, but her body language was brittle with rejection. Of him. Of the past. He prayed for patience. "Gina . . . that night . . . in the garden . . . I'd known for some time that you were struggling. Hurting. I cared about you a great deal, and I should have tried harder to offer my support, but I was so damned wrapped up in my work."

"I wasn't your responsibility." He heard hostility now, and he wondered if it was a cover for something else more truthful.

"Maybe not," he conceded. "But you deserved to have

someone in your corner. Your parents certainly weren't giving you any guidance."

Again, that negligent shrug. "They had their own demons to battle. Still do, for that matter."

This time he touched her cheek, unable to resist the opportunity to see if it was as soft as it looked in the moonlight. "I never meant to hurt you that night, sweetheart. And I should never have said any of those things to you."

Her lips were pressed in a thin line. To keep them from trembling? "You actually did me a favor," she said with a nonchalance he knew was forced. "I needed that figurative smack. I accept your apology and absolve you of all guilt past and present."

Her flippant sarcasm made him want to shake her. But he kept his cool. Barely. "Don't you want to know why I lashed out at you?"

She looked at him then, her eyes shadowed and her expression remote. "Not really. I deserved it. Let's leave it at that."

Dammit. She was throwing up walls again, and he hated them. He shoved his hands in his pockets to keep from reaching for her. He sighed, ready to throw his ego to the winds. "I wanted you, Gina. Badly. And a man in that condition doesn't always make the best decisions. I was ten years older than you were and should have known better. But when we kissed, I got out of control so quickly, I panicked. I was inches away from taking you right then and there."

She was so still, he could hardly tell she was breathing.

When she didn't respond, he beat his fists on the rail. "You had to feel how my body responded to you. I was on the edge. And I chose to attack you verbally rather than give in to the physical intimacy I wanted so badly. It was a stupid mistake, and I'd give anything to be able to take it back."

"You didn't lie." A three-word whisper.

He stroked a hand down her slender arm, needing that intimate touch like a thirsty man needed water. "I was cruel."

She turned to face him then, her arms wrapped around her waist. "I was a silly, lovestruck girl. You were a grown man. It wasn't going to end well."

He cupped her shoulders in his hands, feeling the delicate bones beneath the resilient flesh. "Not a day has passed," he said gruffly, "that I haven't regretted what I missed. You were so beautiful that night, it made me ache."

He didn't plan what happened next. He lowered his head and found her mouth with his. When their lips touched, the shock slammed into him and took his breath. His hands cradled her face.

It all came back in a rush of giddy sensation. He hadn't forgotten the taste of her. The feel of her in his arms. No woman had ever felt so right in his embrace. He wanted to protect and ravage her and grovel humbly at her feet.

His tongue pressed its way into her mouth.

She was stiff at first, but as he murmured words of regret and remorse, she stirred. Her arms came around his neck, and her breasts crushed up against his chest. His hands moved to her tits, caressing them through the thin fabric of her dress.

The nipples pebbled beneath his fingers, and he groaned, swamped with a wave of lust and affection. She was so strong, and yet so terribly vulnerable. And though they were older now, he still couldn't take advantage of her. An apology with a pass was a piss-poor way to make amends.

He released her slowly, calling himself ten kinds of fool. He tried to swallow the lump in his throat. "You still affect me," he said with a harsh, breathless rasp. He owed her honesty, at the very least.

She seemed shell-shocked, much like he felt. Her eyes were huge and dark. She cleared her throat. "After you kissed me that night, I saw disgust on your face." The pain she had carried for six years was in her voice, in her poignant, defensive posture.

It raked across his heart and his conscience like jagged glass. "For myself," he said roughly. "For letting my dick take control when I should have been the man you needed. I was disgusted with my own selfishness. Never with you, Gina. I thought then, and still do, that you were the most amazing woman I've ever known."

"I was a spoiled brat," she whispered.

He smoothed a strand of hair that had escaped to curl at her cheek. "You were a fascinating young woman. I wanted to protect you and to be your lover. But there was no way to do both. In the end, I managed to destroy the possibility of either."

This time *her* hand lifted to touch *his* cheek. It was the first time in six years she had initiated any contact between them, and he held his breath. Her slender fingers were like brands of hot fire against his skin. "So what now?"

He trembled and felt his knees go weak. Three tiny words. Her quiet forgiveness opened up a wealth of ripe possibilities. "Whatever you want, Gina." He meant it literally. He would give her the world if he could. Not because he had wronged her or because she deserved it, but because he cared.

At the moment he was reluctant to analyze what that implied. He'd always cared for Gina. Just because he was almost forty years old and had never married didn't mean anything. Did it? He'd known many women in his life. A good number of those in the biblical sense. He'd simply never found anyone who touched his heart deeply enough for him to want permanence.

He'd known Gina her whole life, and when he kissed her a few moments ago, it was if he had stepped back in time. His feelings for her were as urgent and volatile as they ever were. It frankly shocked him. Surely he hadn't been waiting for her all these years. That would be pretty pathetic. Wouldn't it?

She opened her mouth to say something, and then clearly she thought better of it. She backed away a couple of steps and tried to smile. But he saw the effort it took.

She looked out at the water and then back at him. "Good night, Trey. I'll see you tomorrow."

Gina huddled beneath the covers and cried until her nose was clogged and her head ached. Trey didn't hate her. He was proud of her. Maybe if she repeated the words enough, she would finally begin to believe them.

She felt odd, totally unable to comprehend what had happened in the last twenty-four hours. It was as if a rip in her heart had been repaired and the deep well of shame held over from that one disastrous night had finally been capped.

She wanted to laugh as much as she wanted to cry, but she was afraid to tempt fate. This bubbling feeling of happiness scared her to death. She wasn't accustomed to it, and she feared it might be snatched away in a heartbeat.

She understood pain and confusion and anger, and in recent years she had recognized a measure of contentment. But any real joy in her life had been fleeting. She didn't know how to react.

Trey had wanted to make love to her that long-ago evening. He had cared about her. In light of his confession, she could even begin to understand the harsh, angry words he had tossed at her.

Regardless of his remorse, he had done her a favor that night. The truth, no matter how unpalatable, had smacked her in the face, and that watershed moment had changed her irrevocably.

She might regret the pain of Trey's rejection, but she wouldn't—couldn't—regret the consequences. She was the woman she was today because Trey had been honest enough to mete out the truth.

She closed her eyes and remembered the feel of his lips a little while ago. The first touch of his mouth on hers had been nothing short of cataclysmic. Six years earlier she had loved him with an immature girl's shallow passion.

Now she knew beyond the shadow of a doubt. She had never gotten over him. Well, that wasn't exactly the truth. Deep in her heart, she had always known. But she'd never admitted it to herself. It hurt too much.

She felt giddy and weak with longing. She'd promised Kallie and Catherine she would come on this cruise and have a fun-in-the-sun fling. She'd never had any real intention of doing so. And she would have been willing to lie to conceal the truth.

She didn't have casual sex, because she couldn't have the only man she had ever wanted. Trey Lipman.

Even her two best friends didn't know the whole truth. Gina had graduated from college still a virgin. Her party girl facade had fooled everyone around her, including an army of hopeful guys. Every one of them who dated her abandoned her rather quickly when they discovered she wouldn't put out. And because each thought he was the only one who hadn't been invited into her bed, no one admitted it. Her slutty reputation, false though it was, remained intact.

In late elementary school, she'd developed breasts almost two years before most of her peers. The sudden attention from boys had embarrassed and scared her. Add to that her parents' skewed examples of love and sex, and you found a confused young woman who was afraid to let any male get too close.

When she came home from college after graduation, she had renewed her acquaintance with Trey Lipman. As a longtime friend of the family, she had known him well. She always cherished happy memories of a college-aged Trey being kind to a quiet, unhappy ten-year-old.

But in her early twenties, she was suddenly inundated with feelings that were new and a little scary. She discovered sexual desire for the first time. Trey was nothing at all like the crazy, hound-dog guys who ran in her crowd.

He was mature and focused and so hot he made her ache. In secret places that made her blush. And pant. And yearn.

She had woven silly girlish dreams about him until that one awful night. And what happened next only added to her mountain of shame.

She'd brought a date to the party where she threw herself at Trey. Afterward, she'd been blind with panic and hurt. She'd gone to her date's apartment and given him her virginity. He'd been stinking drunk, and he had hurt her. The only blessing was that because he was so out of it, she'd been able to clean up the evidence of her virginity without his knowing.

She never spoke to him again.

She had been so traumatized by the events of that night that she had finally sought out a counselor, a female professor at her college who had recently gone into private practice.

The woman had been kind and helpful. Over a period of weeks she helped Gina work through the almost unbearable load of guilt she carried. She'd helped her focus on what direction she wanted to go with her life, and she had encouraged Gina to look for men who would respect and care for her.

Gina had tried. Really she had. But big boobs and an even bigger bank balance made it hard to separate the wheat from the chaff. There were a few nice men along the way, but when she realized she didn't have even a smidgen of sexual attraction toward any of them, she let them down as gently as she could.

The jerks, unfortunately, were far more numerous. She had chosen wrong enough times to shake her confidence, and in the last couple of years, she had just about given up. Hence Kallie's and Catherine's insistence on the cruise. They were each blissfully happy, and they were determined to make sure that Gina was as well.

She had actually contemplated having a casual sexual liaison while on board. It would have gone against everything she had learned about herself, but she was lonely, and she wanted to know if she had it in her to be sexual with a man.

Well, Trey Lipman had answered that question. Her dormant libido had roared into life, and she felt as scared and eager and aroused as she had that never-forgotten night when her life had changed so drastically.

He'd left the next move up to her. This might be her only chance to ever get close to him. His kiss clearly said he was still attracted to her. That he would still enjoy having sex with her.

So why not let Trey be her holiday fling? Clearly he wasn't looking for anything more. A handsome, successful straight man didn't get to the age Trey was, and still be unattached, without having some serious commitment issues. Look at George Clooney.

Trey was every bit as dynamic and sexy, and it was obvious that he, too, wasn't interested in marriage. She could live with that. But if she had this one chance to share his bed, would that be enough?

Her inner self said no, but she ignored it. She would live for the moment. She would fulfill her pact with her best friends, and if the fates smiled on her, she would finally know what it was like to make love to the man she had always kept in her heart.

Trey was an early riser. Despite a largely sleepless night, he was up at five thirty. He showered and dressed and went up on deck to enjoy the pristine morning. A faint mist rose off the water far below, and the delicate wispy clouds, what few decorated the sky, were tinted with mauve, pink, and gold.

They had docked overnight in Key West, and soon most of the passengers would begin to disembark. He had some ideas about that, but they required the consent of a certain sexy redhead.

He approached a line of deck chairs, intending to relax and watch the day come to life. The ship had several swimming pools on various decks. The one in front of him was the smallest, and he expected it to be deserted at this hour.

But as he drew closer, a gentle splash caught his ear just

as he noticed one slender arm and then another cleave the water in a slow, graceful backstroke. His heartbeat kicked up a notch and his breath quickened when he recognized the swimmer.

He picked up her towel, settled into a chair near the edge of the pool, and waited. She swam like she did everything else. You could almost see her need to burn off excess energy as she completed lap after lap in quick succession. Her quiet enjoyment of the challenging exercise was evident.

Ten minutes later, she pulled herself out of the water and froze when she saw him sitting there. He stood up and smiled. She was wearing a moss green one-piece suit today. It was cut high on the thigh, low in the back, and modestly scooped at the neckline. Unfortunately for his peace of mind, any modesty the suit possessed was negated by the tempting swells of Gina's breasts.

There was a slight chill in the morning air, and her nipples thrust against the slick, wet fabric. He cleared his throat and kept the towel in front of him.

She held out her hand. "May I have my towel, please?" Her dripping hair, streaming down her back, was a dark ruby red.

He cocked his head. "It would be a shame to cover up all that beauty."

A tiny smile appeared and disappeared. He took it as a minor triumph.

She frowned, but it seemed halfhearted at best. "My towel, Trey."

He stepped behind her and wrapped her in the generous folds of white terry cloth. With his arms around her, he nuzzled her hair. It smelled of coconut and chlorine. He released her reluctantly.

Gina seated herself on the end of a lounge chair and he followed suit on the one nearby, watching as she rummaged in her bag for a large-toothed comb. He let her fumble with the tangles in her long, damp tresses for about a minute and then he scooted behind her, nudging her forward on the seat.

The look she gave him over her shoulder was equal parts surprise and pleasure. It was the vulnerability, though, that caught a raw place in his heart and made him touch her with tenderness rather than hunger.

Carefully, reverently, he worked the comb through her wet hair. Occasionally he touched her shoulder, but for the most part, he kept his distance. His sideways position meant that his hip brushed her bottom once or twice. She didn't seem to notice.

He worked in silence until his curiosity got the better of him. "Do you always exercise so early in the mornings?"

She laughed softly. "Not as a rule. But I decided if I was going to be able to swim without getting burned to a crisp, I had better take advantage of the morning sun. Plus, I like the privacy."

He winced. "Sorry," he muttered.

She reached up and touched his hand, a fleeting caress. "Don't be silly."

It took him fifteen minutes to restore order to her hair.

By then, some sections were already starting to dry. Those strands were light streaks against the darker crimson. The sun made them glint like gold.

His hands began to shake as her nearness worked on him like a drug. Without measuring the risk, he moved and stretched his leg across the lounger until he rested with his back against the seat. Slowly, ready for her resistance, he eased her back into his embrace. Her head settled onto his shoulder as she sighed.

He put his arms around her narrow waist, clasping his hands just below her breasts. If they had been somewhere private, he would have peeled down the straps of her suit and fondled her gorgeous tits.

She had to feel his boner against her butt. There was nothing he could do to hide it. Nor did he want to. He needed her to know, to feel, to see how much he still wanted her.

Her hands rested lightly on his thighs. He had on khaki shorts and leather deck shoes. Seeing her slim, pale fingers against his darker, hair-covered leg made him tremble.

But soon, voices and people appeared, and the sun rose overhead with merciless heat. He kissed her cheek. "Let's get you inside, or at least covered up."

He helped her to her feet with a wince of regret. He would have been happy to sit there for hours, just holding her.

She gathered up her things and put on her sunglasses. Now he couldn't read her expression.

He traced her collarbone with a fingertip. "Would you like to explore Key West?"

She nodded, her lips curved in a half smile. "Of course. I'll meet you at the departure ramp in forty-five minutes."

Gina showered and changed, with her heart skipping and jumping like a young girl's. It was a disconcerting feeling. Most of the time she felt old beyond her years. She wasn't accustomed to this sensation of giddy anticipation.

She dressed in white capri pants and a turquoise and white tank top with a sheer, long-sleeve collared shirt on top. The thin fabric wouldn't be too hot, and it would give her a bit of protection from the sun.

She tucked what she would need for the day in a raffia tote and sprayed a dab of Romance at her throat and wrists. She glanced in the mirror. The sparkle in her eyes brought her up short.

Was she headed for a fall? It was one thing to contemplate having sex with Trey Lipman. But she'd be insane to deliberately invite heartache by building silly, girlish castles in the air.

She was smarter than that. She had learned how to protect herself. It had been a tough lesson, and she'd do well to remember it before she made a fool of herself.

Now the unsmiling woman in the mirror looked more familiar. Sober. Guarded. Immune to life's nasty surprises.

With a sigh, she gathered up her things and headed for the door.

Three

Trey hovered near the ship rail and checked his watch. Gina wasn't late. He was merely anxious. When she appeared around the corner moments later, he sucked in a breath. He still hadn't quite adjusted to the impact her beauty had on his very susceptible libido. When she was near him, everything in his body went hard and taut with hunger.

She looked cool and elegant, like a movie star . . . maybe Sophia Loren. Her sunglasses shaded her eyes, so he couldn't read much from her expression. But her lips tilted in a small smile when she joined him.

He slung an arm around her shoulders, unable to resist touching her. "Ready to try your land legs?" Her skin was soft and warm beneath the thin fabric of her top.

She rested her cheek against his arm for one brief wonderful second and then straightened her spine. "Of course."

They had breakfast at a streetside café on Duval. The coffee and croissants were excellent, but the best part of the alfresco meal was the opportunity to people watch. The tourists from the ship were easy to spot. But the locals were far more interesting.

Well, to be honest . . . Gina watched the people. Trey watched her. She was relaxed and happy at the moment, and though she was always beautiful, in this setting she glowed. Her unconscious sexuality fit perfectly with the tropical ambience of Key West.

The flowers, the colors, the quirky characters, the warm sun. Everything seemed brighter and more vibrant here. He loved Charleston and all its many charms. But if his hometown was a genteel Southern lady, Key West was a bawdy Mae West. Blatant in its quest for enjoyment and the laid-back easy life.

He paid the check and quirked an eyebrow. "I have a surprise for you, if you're game."

Her forehead wrinkled in suspicion, but Gina wasn't the type to back down from a challenge. "Sure. Whatever. I'll let you be the boss . . . today."

His cock flexed, sensing a sexual gauntlet. Was he imagining things, or was pretty Gina giving him the green light for a more intimate slate of activities? He shivered, caught up in the erotic possibilities flitting through his brain.

Gina made some comment, and he forced himself to pay attention. He took her arm as they wandered down toward the waterfront. The crowds weren't that heavy, but it was an acceptable excuse to touch her. They skirted to the right of the big fancy hotels and headed to the crowded marina.

Boats of every kind bobbed in the water. Tall-masted

schooners, sleek yachts, speedy catamarans. He motioned toward a sign. "Are you interested in snorkeling? They do a half-day trip that would get us back in time."

Gina shuddered theatrically. "No thanks. I'd rather not make it too easy for the sharks."

He laughed. "You'd love it, I promise, but we'll save that for another day."

He'd tossed out the remark carelessly, but he tried to gauge her reaction. He was way ahead of her probably. He was assuming this edgy attraction was going somewhere. And his determination to make damn sure it did surprised even him.

Gina made no discernible response to his casual comment. She was looking around with interest, taking in all the bustle of activity.

He steered her toward a small wooden kiosk. She skidded to a sudden stop, her face blanching as she read the information board. "Oh, no, Trey. I don't think so. You go. I'll wander around for a bit."

He urged her forward. "Parasailing is great. I promise. And I swear it's not at all scary. Honest."

Her fingernails dug into his forearm. "Then why is my heart doing somersaults?"

He gave her a quick kiss, loving her wry self-deprecation. "Maybe because you're with a handsome man," he teased.

She grimaced. "Oh, yeah, that's it."

He could feel the tension in her body the entire time she stood beside him as he stepped up to the counter and made the arrangements. As he tucked his credit card back inside his billfold, he gave her an encouraging grin. "Chin up, Gina. They haven't lost a single passenger this year."

She gave him a dirty look, and he slid an arm around her waist, laughing. "Come on, scaredy cat. Our boat's this way. They usually take three couples out for an hour, and each gets a brief ride, but I paid more so we could have longer."

Her sunglasses were tucked on top of her head for the moment because they had been standing in the shade. She shot him a death look. "Oh, great. More time to be dangled over the great ocean of death."

He was still chuckling when they boarded the small white craft with the outboard motor. His smile faded when he saw how the two crew guys looked at Gina. They both had identical shell-shocked, goofy grins on their faces, and their eyes were locked on her chest.

Each was blond and in his mid-twenties. They were shirtless and tanned, and their abs were hard enough to make any woman drool. Trey was left to fend for himself as the two fell all over each other to help Gina into the boat and make her comfortable.

He watched in amusement as she charmed them effortlessly. Underneath, she was probably still petrified, but she would never let on in front of an audience.

Donning life jackets was interesting. Crew guy number one was all thumbs, trying to adjust the straps to accommodate Gina's ample breasts. Trey lost his smile when the guy's hands strayed once too often. But by that time, Gina had already shooed him away with a pleasant smile and was finishing the job on her own.

They pushed off and moved slowly in and among the tightly packed vessels, observing the NO WAKE signs until they were clear of the harbor. He watched as Gina retrieved a white cotton sun hat from her bag and pulled it over her hair. Without asking for permission, he helped her tuck the loose strands under the brim.

Then just for the hell of it, he pulled her close and kissed her hard, his tongue probing deep in her mouth. She tasted like orange marmalade.

She went still in his embrace, and he wondered if she was embarrassed by his PDA. He released her reluctantly, debating whether she would have been amenable to renting a romantic suite at the Hilton and spending the afternoon in bed. His body reacted predictably to that idea, and he was glad his khaki shorts were roomy.

If the two younger men were impressed by his Neanderthal posturing, they didn't show it. While one guy steered out into open water, the other one held Gina's arm and started helping her into the harness.

Trey was damned glad she hadn't been willing to expose her fair skin in shorts, because the guy's wandering hands were all over her butt and legs. Gina was laughing breathlessly and talking a mile a minute. Her eyes were huge.

He gave her an encouraging smile as he slipped into the other side of the tandem harness. "Relax. We'll take it nice and easy." She didn't look at all convinced.

When all the buckles and straps were adjusted, checked, and rechecked, he and Gina sat back on the flat portion of the boat, their legs extended straight out in front. The green Astroturf-type covering beneath them scratched his calves. To their backs, the colorful yellow and crimson sail lay crumpled carefully, ready to catch the wind when the time came.

Crew guy was explaining to Gina what would happen . . . how the boat would accelerate, the rope would extend, and she and Trey would simply lift slowly into the air.

Trey took her hand, and her long, slender fingers twined around his in a death grip. He nudged her shoulder. "I won't let anything happen to you, Gina. You trust me, right?"

She inhaled, her smile shaky. "I trust *you*. It's the other stuff that has me worried."

Without fanfare, their bottoms lifted free of the deck, and suddenly they were airborne. Gina screeched and squeezed her eyes shut. Above them, the sail billowed and snapped taut.

He touched her knee. "Watch, Gina. You've got to see this."

She whimpered but opened one eye and looked down. They were gaining altitude rapidly, but there was little or no sensation of speed. Her mouth opened in a silent *O* of appreciation. He saw her eyes widen as she realized how high they already were. Below them, the water was so clear you could see all the way to the bottom of the ocean. Greens and browns and a dozen shades of blue from aquamarine to navy. Boats and Jet Skis were little dots on the liquid landscape.

All of Key West stretched before them, angling back to the long chain of islands that led toward the mainland. The awe on her face made him fiercely glad he had pushed her a bit.

He scanned the limitless horizon and relished the sensation of privacy. They were suspended in perfect intimacy far above the earth. "Well, what do you think? Is it how you imagined?"

Her eyes were glued to the breathtaking panorama below. "It doesn't even seem like we're very high," she said softly. "We're just floating . . ." Her voice trailed off, and the wonder in her whispered words made him want to kiss her again.

Paying for the extra time had been a stroke of genius. Silence stretched between them, warm and comfortable, as they took it all in. Not only were they free of interruptions, but Gina was literally bound to his side. He allowed her another long minute to enjoy the view, and then he probed gently. "So why is Gina McCutcheon on a cruise in January?"

The pleasure faded from her face, and he could have kicked himself. "Doesn't it suit my party girl image?" She wasn't looking at him, but he caught the sarcastic bite in her voice dead-on.

He winced, realizing he had unwittingly shattered the mood. "Stop it, Gina. You don't need to do that with me, not anymore."

She shrugged, her jaw tight. "Do what?"

"Play the spoiled princess."

"It's what people expect."

"Even now? With all you've accomplished? That doesn't seem fair."

"Now, whoever told you life was fair, Mr. Lipman?" Her words were sharp and cynical and cold as ice.

His stomach clenched. "I'm sorry if life has been unkind to you, Gina. And I'm even more sorry that *I* hurt you."

Her lips tightened. "Really, Trey. I have nothing to complain about. I have money to burn. Didn't you know? Money fixes everything."

She was hurting deep inside, and he felt powerless to do anything about it. Suddenly he cursed the damned constraints. He twisted awkwardly, managing to capture her face between his hands. He kissed her roughly, trying to express what it was too soon to put into words. Finally, her stiff, brittle posture melted, and she responded. Her tongue tangled with his, and she sighed.

One of her hands was on his thigh. The other curled around his neck. He was so hard, he ached. His hands went to her breasts, and he palmed them with a groan of satisfaction. She didn't try to stop him when he slid beneath her clothing, pushed up her bra, and found bare skin.

The weight of her tits in his palms made him dizzy. He teased the nipples with his thumbs. Her shuddering response made him bolder. He pinched her tight buds and made himself crazy imagining what it would be like when he first tasted them. Oh, god.

He kissed her throat . . . nuzzled the lovely indentation

between her breasts. The scent of her skin affected him like a drug. She tilted her head back as he nibbled his way up to her chin.

They both jerked and laughed as her hat flew from her head. They grabbed for it simultaneously, but it fell in graceful arcs, tumbling on the wind currents like a small white bird.

He ran his fingers through her hair. "I'll buy you another one," he murmured, kissing her forehead, her eyelids, her cheeks.

She pulled his head closer. "I don't want another hat, Trey. I want you."

His heart fell from his chest, chasing the hat far below. He was light-headed. He had never dared hope she would state her intentions so plainly. If at all. Six years ago she had wanted him, but a lot had changed since then.

He pulled back, swallowing hard and wiping his damp forehead with the back of his hand. "You can have both," he said mildly, trying to act as if his world hadn't just skidded out of control.

She straightened her top and smiled ruefully. "How much time do we have left?"

He glanced at his watch. "About ten minutes." He held her right hand in his left one. "As great as this is, I'm about ready to get out of this stupid harness. It's like a damned chastity belt."

She grinned. "You just don't like having your smooth moves compromised."

He lifted an eyebrow. "Smooth moves? I'm no operator, Gina. I'm just a regular guy trying to impress a beautiful woman."

She snorted, her lovely profile reflecting innocent contentment. "You may be a workaholic, but I've kept up with your escapades. Women line up at your door. Don't try to deny it."

He was silent for a moment. It was sobering to realize how different the last six years might have been if he'd had even a modicum of self-control where Gina was concerned.

He cleared his throat. "I don't think this is a very productive conversation." He squeezed her fingers. "You never did tell me. Why a cruise?"

She sighed, watching a nearby seaplane circle to land. "Well . . . Kallie and Catherine are a lot like your dear grandmother. They bullied me into it."

"Ah."

"All three of us will turn thirty in a few months."

He grinned. "I know. But it didn't seem polite to mention it."

"Yeah, thanks."

Her smart-ass comeback made him laugh. "Go on. Don't keep me in suspense."

"On our twenty-ninth birthdays we all made a pact to act on a secret, hidden fantasy in the upcoming year. For Catherine, that was Phillip."

"And Kallie was in love with Beau."

"Exactly."

"I heard about the double wedding plans." He saw a wince flit across her face.

"Yeah. They're very happy."

"What about you, Gina? What was your secret, naughty fantasy?"

She evaded his gaze, pointedly looking down at the boat far below them. "Shouldn't they be reeling us in by now?"

"Quit stalling."

"I didn't have one." She said it bluntly, as though daring him to argue. "I promised them I would find a gorgeous man on this cruise and get laid."

Trey scowled inwardly. He didn't like the sound of that. Was he simply a means to an end as far as she was concerned? "I see."

She muttered something under her breath. "I lied to my two best friends. I doubt you'll believe me, but I haven't had sex in a couple of years. And I didn't plan to do the horizontal hokeypokey on this cruise. But they're both so deliriously happy, I had to do something to get them to leave me alone."

He frowned, feeling the tug as the crewman below began lowering them a bit at a time. He was running out of opportunities to worm the truth out of her faster than he was losing rope. "First of all, Gina, I will always believe anything you tell me. Period. I never believed you had sex with all those guys back then, no matter how convincingly you played the party girl. I knew you. I know you. You aren't promiscuous."

Her face was still turned away. "I did think seriously about it . . . having sex on this cruise, I mean," she admitted. "I'm young, and I have needs like anybody else."

"But?"

"But it was too much work. Flirting. Playing the game. Feeling let down afterward. I decided it would be easier to take the stupid cruise, invent a hunky guy, and go home with a vague romantic tale of tropical passion and satisfied lust."

Gina realized with a sigh of relief that they were almost down to the boat. The two crewmen grinned as they deliberately lowered their passengers ankle-deep in the choppy ocean, causing Gina to squeak in alarm. Seconds later they popped them back up and gently brought them in to let their feet touch down on the deck.

She never even stumbled. In the hustle and bustle of unfastening buckles and stepping out of the harness, she was able to ignore Trey for a moment. She was still vaguely in shock. She had practically propositioned him god knows how high above the water.

Of course, in all fairness, he did have his tongue down her throat and his fingers on her nipples. That was enough to addle any woman's brain. If he didn't think she was easy, it was no credit to her. She'd practically climbed into his lap.

Not to mention the fact that she had casually mentioned she wanted him. That was subtle.

Her face burning despite the powerful sunscreen, she

thanked their instructors and watched as Trey tipped them generously. One of them popped a small memory card from his camera and handed it to Trey.

She was aghast. "They took pictures?" Lord knows what they were able to see from below.

Trey grinned, reading her discomfiture accurately. "Mostly just on takeoff and landing. I paid for them when we signed up. I thought you might like a memento of our trip."

The hot, male appreciation in his gaze sparked an answering blaze deep in her stomach. Her sex clenched, and she wanted to rip off all her clothes and dive into the ocean, despite the fact that water and she didn't get along. At least not scary, murky water uncontained by tubs or pools. Right now she might be willing to make an exception.

They thanked the two young men and made their goodbyes. On the dock, Trey took her arm. The midday sun beamed down without mercy, despite the fact it was January. She felt wilted. Trey, on the other hand, still looked as fresh and clean-cut as he had at six a.m.

His khaki shorts had a sharp crease and his short-sleeve navy oxford cloth shirt had nary a wrinkle. It really wasn't fair.

He touched the tip of her nose. "You're getting pink."

"I'll put more sunscreen on after lunch."

"So what now?"

"A bathroom, a cold drink, and something light to eat."

He took her bag and slung it over his shoulder. "I think we can manage that."

The hours that followed were flirting, and foreplay, and the renewal of a friendship Gina had dearly missed, all in one magical, breathtakingly tender afternoon. She dropped her emotional barriers. He shed his workaholic ways. They ate and laughed and shopped and played and, through it all, sexual energy and anticipation hummed and sparked between them.

It frightened her a bit to realize how much she still cared about him. Had she ever stopped? That encounter in the garden a half-dozen years ago wouldn't have hurt so badly if she hadn't been halfway in love with him even then.

She'd worked hard to prove to the world that she had changed, that she had grown up. But maybe the one person she'd really been trying to impress all along was the man with the easy smile, the broad shoulders, and the eyes that saw past her prickly defenses to the woman who yearned to be loved.

Her heart stopped dead in her chest for a split second and then pounded sluggishly. My god, was she in love with Trey Lipman? She certainly had been back then. If you could call it love. At twenty-three, she hadn't really known what the word meant. Not between a man and a woman. But despite their estrangement, she had never been able to get Trey out of her mind.

She had followed his career and his well-documented social life. She'd kept up with his family. In everything she did, in the back of her mind, there was always the question . . . *What would Trey think of this?*

She was stunned. No wonder none of the guys she dated had ever measured up. She'd been comparing them all to Trey.

It would be suicide to let herself start weaving hazy fantasies now. Trey was not a marrying man. He had a career and a string of nonpermanent sexual partners. Apparently, at the present moment, he was amenable to the idea of a shipboard fling with her.

But all bets were off when they docked back in Miami. He had his life. She had hers. Suddenly, every bit of the day's champagne sparkle faded, and she felt raw and tired and sad.

At that moment, Trey tucked her beneath a pretty umbrella at an outdoor table and purchased her an icy cold lemonade. "Drink this," he said abruptly. "I'll be right back."

She watched, still lost in thought, as he disappeared into one of the numerous high-end jewelry stores nearby. She recognized the name. A friend had brought her a catalog from one of their properties in Sanibel last year.

He was gone for quite awhile, but she didn't mind. She needed a few minutes to regain her equilibrium. She had no reason to be gloomy. She was going to share Trey Lipman's bed. Probably tonight. And she had a hunch he knew what he was doing between the sheets.

So what if this was a onetime thing? People did it all the time. Recreational sex. That was the term . . . right? Sheer carnal pleasure just for the hell of it. No more, no less.

He appeared suddenly by her side, making her jump. She'd been so lost in thought, she didn't see him return. He sat down beside her on the concrete bench. "This is for you," he said simply. "To commemorate our day in Key West. Go ahead. Open it."

She took the small, shiny black bag with the gold lettering in trembling fingers. The rectangular box inside matched the bag. She removed the lid and the cotton and smiled. On a delicate gold box chain hung a tiny palm tree with three diamond coconuts.

She touched it with a fingertip. "It's lovely, Trey." But it was also far more expensive than it appeared. She'd seen similar charms before. The gift seemed a bit extravagant for a first date. She nibbled her lower lip. "I don't know what to say."

He lifted it from the box. "You don't have to say anything," he muttered, moving her hair and fastening the chain around her neck. His fingers brushed her nape, making her shiver. "There. Perfect."

He sat back, and their eyes met. Unspoken words passed between them. The air was hushed and still. Like in a slow-motion movie reel, they each leaned forward.

His lips were firm and warm and masculine. She made a little noise in her throat and pressed closer, wrapping her arms around his neck. He smelled like lime and sea air and warm starched cotton. "I love it," she murmured, exploring his mouth lazily, shuddering as his tongue dueled with hers.

They were on a public street, surrounded by people, but oblivious to them all. Trey's embrace was chaste, though his kiss was not. His rough voice scraped over her ragged emotions. "I want to make love to you tonight, Gina. Please.

I've wanted you for at least a decade. Put me out of my misery."

She chuckled hoarsely. "It would be my pleasure, Mr. Lipman. Just as long as you know that once won't be enough. I've been saving up, and you're the lucky man."

Four

Trey's ears were ringing, and his hands were shaking. Everything south of his belt was so fucking hard, he had a difficult time standing up.

He held out a hand to Gina. She took it, smiling at him with the kind of look that had been bringing men to their knees since the dawn of time.

Her lips were shiny and wet from their last kiss. Her cheeks were flushed, her pupils dilated in irises that were hazy with arousal.

He licked his lips, trying to forget that the Hilton was only half a block away. "Ready to go back to the ship?" His voice sounded like he had swallowed a bucket of broken seashells.

She nodded, her lashes fluttering down to shield her eyes. "Sure."

Somehow they made it back to the dock and up the gangway. On the deck that led to their cabins, he debated the merits of rushing her back to his room, stripping her naked, and shoving his cock between her fabulous legs without delay.

It was a tempting plan. But hell, this would be their first time. Even the most nonromantic jerk on the planet knew that such a momentous and potentially delicate occasion merited some finesse.

God, he hoped he had packed some. And condoms. Shit. Did he have any condoms? He normally kept them in his shaving kit, but he certainly hadn't anticipated needing them on this trip. The ship's store. That was it. He'd have time to purchase a case of them before dinner. His forehead was sweating, and his stomach churned.

He must have looked strange, because Gina cocked her head and was studying his face. "Are you okay, Trey?" The wicked little half smile she wore told him that she suspected at least a portion of his emotional and physical upheaval.

He cleared his throat. "Yeah. Never better." He stuttered to a halt and glanced at his watch. "Guess we'd better clean up and change for dinner."

She went up on tiptoe and plastered her body against his, sliding her arms around his waist and kissing him hungrily. He moaned and pulled her even closer. When every last brain cell he could claim had settled in his groin, she pulled away. "Pick me up at seven."

He nodded jerkily, watching her walk away with an unconscious sway to her hips that attracted every male gaze in a hundred-yard radius.

He stumbled back to his room and stripped off his

clothes. Beneath the punishing spray of an icy cold shower, he imagined Gina's slender fingers wrapped around his shaft, her bare tits glistening wet. He palmed his cock and jerked off, groaning and shuddering when he came in hot, jerky spurts.

Afterward he dried off and tumbled onto the bed. He had time for a fifteen-minute power nap, and he had a feeling he was going to need it.

Gina floated around her cabin, humming as she combed out her freshly washed hair and debated what to wear. Tonight was the formal dinner, and Trey would be in a tux. Thinking about it made her knees weak.

Just because they hadn't spoken more than a dozen words in six years didn't mean their paths hadn't collided. They moved in the same social circles, and she'd seen him across any number of crowded rooms. He had a commanding presence that was hard to ignore, no matter how much she tried.

Tonight she wouldn't be avoiding him. Tonight she would be in his arms and in his bed. She sat on the edge of the mattress as her knees gave out. Trey. Naked. Making love to her. *Sweet lord.* She hoped her rusty sexual skills were up to the challenge.

By the time she had finished her toilette, it was a quarter till seven. She had used a bit more makeup than usual, and in the mirror her eyes looked enormous. She'd dusted a bit of glittery powder in her cleavage, and the fragrance of perfume on her warm skin made her think of sex. So did the dampness between her legs, her pointed nipples, and the shaky tremor in her breathing.

She'd been humming for the last hour. *Humming.* For godsakes. What had he done to her? Gina McCutcheon was a hard-ass. A sharp-edged, savvy, don't-mess-with-me female. She didn't even recognize the woman in the mirror. The dewy skin, the soft eyes, the trembling lips.

That woman bore a striking resemblance to the naive, love-starved twenty-three-year-old, cruising for a fall, who had thrown herself at a very sophisticated, sexy Trey Lipman. A shiver of remembered pain tightened her lips. But she shook off her misgivings. Tonight was her night. Hers and Trey's. The past was over and finished. From here on out, it was new ground.

Trey straightened the sleeves of his jacket and knocked at Gina's cabin door. She answered immediately, joined him in the corridor, and locked up. She handed him her key and a slender gold tube of lipstick. "Do you mind?"

He tucked them in his pocket, trying to speak through numb lips. She looked amazing. Her dress was white tonight. Some kind of thin cotton with spaghetti straps and an uneven handkerchief-hem skirt. It was lined, surely, but he could swear he saw the dark outline of her nipples through the snug bodice.

On her narrow feet, she wore drop-dead sexy gold sandals that were little more than narrow straps and at least four-inch heels. They made her closer to his height, and eminently kissable.

In the smooth curve of her cleavage, his gift nestled, taunting him with its precarious position on the slopes of her lush breasts. Her masses of red-bronze hair tumbled across her shoulders.

He took her cool hand in his warm one. "Come on, gorgeous. I'm starving."

Despite his claim, he couldn't recall what they ate that evening. It must have been wonderful, because their dinner companions were vocal in their appreciation. Every man at the table, regardless of age or sexual orientation, noticed Gina's shimmering sexuality.

She was like an exotic island orchid, fresh and rare and delicate. Beneath the table, his hand stroked her knee, brushing aside the folds of her skirt to touch her bare skin.

He caught her by surprise once, noting her little exhalation of breath, the slight widening of her eyes, the way she squirmed in her seat.

His prick was so hard, he ached. He couldn't remember the last time he'd felt this level of arousal. Maybe never. Or maybe it was the last time he held a younger Gina in a secluded garden and felt the sweet taste of her mouth against his, the warm press of her tits against his chest.

He talked and laughed and made conversation like some damned animatronic puppet. Over dessert, peaches flambé, he allowed his questing fingers to slide higher on a sleek, toned thigh. Gina stiffened. He leaned in for a quick, affectionate kiss, vaguely aware of the indulgent smiles of their dinner companions. Everyone loved a romance. He wondered if they thought he and Gina were on their honeymoon.

That random thought hit him square in the chest. Gina. Marriage. The idea should have shocked him. But it didn't. It settled in his brain like a welcome fall of rain on parched earth. Gina. His bride. Tucked in his bed every night. Laughing with him. Loving him. He glanced at his wineglass, trying to remember how many times the steward had refilled it. Not more than twice, surely.

The captain made a brief announcement about dancing in the lounge, and he and Gina allowed themselves to be pulled along in the crush of people headed that direction. On the dance floor, he drew her into his arms, grateful for the socially acceptable occasion to hold her close.

She fit in his embrace like the long-awaited final piece of a puzzle. Everywhere he touched on her body made his knees weak and his cock hard. The smooth plane of her back. Her narrow waist. Her slender shoulders. The beautiful curve of her neck.

They moved in perfect rhythm, losing track of the hours. Her head rested on his shoulder, her gentle breath brushing the sensitive skin of his throat. His fingers traced her spine and toyed with the top of her zipper. "I have an idea," he said gruffly.

"Hmmm?" She didn't open her eyes. A faint smile tilted her mouth.

"How does a late-night swim sound to you? We'd have that top-deck pool all to ourselves at this hour."

Her head tilted back as she looked at him, her cheeks streaked with color. He pressed a kiss beneath her ear. "I thought it might cool me off," he confessed, groaning as her fingertips caressed the nape of his neck.

She kissed his cheek. "I like you hot."

His knees almost buckled. "Gina." It was the only word he could squeeze past his almost paralyzed vocal cords.

She hugged him close and released him. "I'll meet you there in fifteen minutes."

His jaw locked. His hands clenched at his sides. He struggled to breathe. "Make it ten."

She disappeared in a flash of white into the crowd. He dashed to his cabin, tossed his dress clothes aside, and pulled on a pair of swim trunks. He shrugged into a loose-fitting shirt, slid his feet into deck shoes, and raced up the stairs.

She made it in twelve. She had her raffia tote in hand. Her hair was pulled up in a knot on top of her head, and she was wearing a thin, gauzy elastic-waist skirt. The buttons on her cover-up were partially open, revealing the top of her turquoise bikini. She dropped the bag with a thud.

As he had suspected, the pool was deserted. Even the lights had been extinguished. It was probably forbidden to swim at this hour, but he couldn't care less.

He held out a hand. "Shall we?"

She stepped out of her skirt and unbuttoned her shirt. Her swimsuit was simple but devastating. The top was nothing more that two miniscule triangles, and the bottom was open on the sides, held together by small, linked circles of rhinestones.

He cleared his throat. "Very pretty."

He abandoned her long enough to dive into the deep end and surface with a flick of his head and a rough laugh. The water felt like warm silk.

Gina stepped decorously down the ladder, slipping into the pool gracefully and lifting her face to the moon overhead. He swam closer, pulled by a force stronger than his self-control.

He slid his arms around her waist, and her legs tangled with his. His stiff erection pressed against her belly. Her eyes were wide in the dim light.

He kissed her softly. "This is nice."

She chuckled. "And for that, I grant you the title Mr. Understatement."

"Don't mock me, Gina, sweetheart. It's hard to find words."

He'd meant it to sound joking, but it came out far too serious.

Her face softened. "I am so happy to be here with you, Trey. And I lied to you earlier. I *did* have a fantasy. But I was afraid to admit it, because it seemed so far-fetched."

His hands lowered to her curvy hips. His fingers trespassed beneath the edge of her bikini bottoms. "And now?" he asked hoarsely.

She wrapped her legs around his waist, making him groan. She pulled his head down for a surprisingly sweet kiss, her lips moving over his in caressing little sweeps. "If I'm dreaming, I don't want to wake up."

He shuddered and brought his hands to her face, angling her chin and capturing her mouth with rough urgent strokes of his tongue. He released her long enough to run his thumbs over the wet fabric covering her tight, hard nipples.

When that wasn't enough, he backed her against the wall of the pool and reached between her legs to stroke her there. She gasped and moved against his hand. Gently, he thrust the narrow strip of cloth aside and entered her with two fingers.

She was wet and hot and tight. He dropped his forehead to hers, realizing in sudden despair that the two dozen condoms he'd purchased earlier were as far away as the moon and back. He gritted his teeth as searing hunger tightened his thighs and swelled his cock even more.

He was breathing like a marathon runner. "Gina, my love. Do I need to get—?"

She shook her head in a vehement negative.

He'd have fallen to his knees in thanksgiving if it wouldn't have drowned them both.

He sucked in a raw breath and ripped the fabric down her legs. One set of the rhinestone circles snapped, making the rest practically useless. He dropped the wet handful of fabric at the edge of the pool. He wanted her to bare her breasts, but even in a sex-starved haze, he knew it wasn't wise in such a setting, despite the hour.

He shoved his trunks partway down his thighs and freed his prick. Deliberately, he used his hands to spread her wide, letting the water slide against every inch of her bare sex. She whimpered and sank her teeth into his shoulder.

Her eyes were closed. Her chest rose and fell with every mesmerizing breath she took. He spared one last look around them to make sure they were alone. Then he centered the head of his cock in her slick folds and pressed deep. She buried her face in his chest as she cried out.

He was standing in shoulder-deep water, barely keeping his balance, with Gina's arms around his neck in a death grip, and his orgasm seconds away. He worked in and out once slowly, trying to stave off the imminent explosion. Awkwardly, he reached between their joined bodies and found her clit. He stroked it gently, feeling Gina shiver in his arms.

He whispered words in her ear, desperate, aching. "I want to feel you come. I want to feel your body milk me and drain me until I can't bear it." He continued murmuring naughty, erotic suggestions as he fondled her intimately.

Suddenly, her back bowed and she groaned from deep in her chest, gasping and sobbing as she climaxed in wave after wave of blinding sensation.

He held her tightly until her body went limp, and then, with a muffled roar, he grabbed her hips and thrust upward again and again until his own orgasm ripped through him and emptied him in a rush of searing heat.

He never really knew how he managed to stay on his feet. He was reluctant to separate their bodies, but he knew the longer they stayed like this, the riskier it was. With a grimace of loss, he slipped from her, supporting her carefully as he stepped into shallower water.

Her eyes were dazed, her lips swollen from his ravenous kisses.

He adjusted his own swimsuit and picked up her bikini bottom with a rueful grin. Only a single small circle remained intact on the left side. He helped her step into it, then hopped out of the pool to grab a big, soft towel.

As Gina climbed up the ladder, he tucked it around her in case anyone was watching. She slipped into her skirt and cover-up while he dried off.

After he was no longer dripping wet, he took her hand and pulled her down onto a lounge chair with him. He put his arms around her waist and urged her back against his chest. He wanted to say something, but he was speechless. Gina seemed equally affected.

His thumb found the pulse in her wrist. It was racketing away as madly as his own. He kissed the side of her neck and heard her say something. Softly. Almost as though she was speaking to herself.

He bent his head, burying his nose in the fragrant hair above her ear. "What, angel?"

She took his hands and deliberately placed them over her breasts. "I want to do it again."

Gina was never able to recall exactly how they made it from the top deck to her cabin. It involved walking like regular people, chatting with the occasional passenger, and smiling normally. They must have succeeded, because when she looked around, still somewhat dazed, they were standing near her bed. Trey locked the door with a loud click, and now he approached her like a hungry lion, his eyes filled with carnal intent, his sensual mouth set in lines of determination.

He stopped two feet away, the heat from his body reaching her even still.

He slipped off his shirt and tossed it aside. His arms folded across his broad chest. "Take off your clothes."

The blunt command sent molten heat pulsing into every swollen, well-used inch of her sex. She clenched her thighs, feeling the sweet honeyed arousal build again. She raised an eyebrow, feigning indignation despite her blinding urge to please. "I beg your pardon?"

"Strip, Gina. Now."

He watched her with hooded eyes to see if she would obey. Slowly she slid her skirt down her legs and removed her top. As she unfastened the two tiny damp pieces of cloth at her hips, she felt the pleasant sting of vulnerability.

His eyes roved from her breasts to her bare-waxed mound and back. He heaved in a breath and exhaled. Tiny streaks of color slashed his cheekbones. "Stand in front of the mirror."

She did as he commanded, moving on shaky legs to position herself before the large lighted vanity. Behind her, she saw Trey's reflection as he extinguished all the lights save for one dim bulb in the bathroom.

He came back to her and stood behind her, his breath warm on her nape. Slowly, his hands came up, and he cupped her breasts. He plumped them and fondled them and pulled at her aching nipples, seemingly fascinated with every nuance of their weight and resilience.

The mirror recorded the erotic tableau faithfully. His hands were dark against her fair skin. They skated lower, caressing her hip bones. He fell to his knees, his face pressed against her ass.

She flinched when his teeth bit gently at first one cheek and then the other. She moved restlessly, feeling moisture gather and dribble from her sex. His hand spread her legs from behind and played with her labia.

Her face in the mirror was blurred with passion, or perhaps her vision was impaired by the creeping, seductive pleasure that was making it difficult to remain upright. She felt his fingers press deep in her vagina, and she moaned.

His thumb made lazy circles on her clitoris. He knew exactly where and how to touch her. Knew the exact combination of strokes and movements to make her weak. He turned her to face him and lifted her to the counter. He crouched and pressed his lips to her center, licking and sucking until she whimpered and writhed.

Her back slumped against the cold glass of the mirror, and her knees lolled apart as splinters of fire radiated from her core.

She was so close. But he stopped short of the goal. Deliberately, it seemed. The front of his swim trunks tented in such a way that his arousal was a given. She'd not been able to see him in the water. She couldn't see him now.

It didn't seem fair.

But the intricacies of right and wrong were lost on her when he dragged her from the vanity and into his arms. He carried her to the plump leather armchair and lowered her headfirst over the high arm.

She heard the rustle of cloth, and a half second later felt the blunt intrusion of his penis entering her from behind. Her hands gripped the chair cushion, her fingernails scoring the leather.

She was dizzy. The sensation of being stretched was indescribable. His powerful lovemaking had been blunted earlier by the resistance of the water.

Now he entered her forcefully, shaking her pliant body with each rapid thrust. Her clitoris rubbed against the arm of the chair, her inner muscles gripped his shaft, and suddenly her world exploded as she climaxed in a shivering, bone-melting crisis of pure, incandescent sensation.

He reached his own satisfaction with a harsh shout, and then he collapsed on top of her, panting and shaking.

Her legs felt like cooked spaghetti when he finally brought them both to their feet. He carried her again, this time pulling back the covers on the bed and then lowering her gently and sliding beside her.

She got her first glance at his cock and sighed in appreciation.

Trey's wise-ass grin told her he knew exactly what she was thinking.

She circled him with one hand and squeezed. His smile disappeared abruptly, and his eyelids fluttered shut. He was still semierect. She stroked him several times and felt his shaft pulse and thicken.

With careful, steady strokes she brought him back to life. His penis was beautiful, as proud and strong as the man himself. She straddled his waist, lowering her body until she could take him deep.

The need to merge with him, to join their bodies in the most intimate way possible, held her on the knife edge of yet another orgasm. She didn't know it was possible to feel this way. She felt as drunk as a kid in a candy store with too much allowance and too many choices.

She raked his nipples with her fingernails, watching in fascination as the muscles in his neck corded and strained. She reached behind her to fondle his balls. They were warm in her hands.

Trey's chest was beautiful, as well. She would have studied it in detail if he hadn't flexed his hips and driven himself an inch deeper.

She gasped and rotated her hips, dragging a curse from between his clenched teeth. She leaned forward, pressing her breasts to his face. The new position did interesting things to the building heat between her legs and had the added advantage of making her nipples available for sucking.

Trey needed no further invitation. He bit down gently on one and held an arm tightly across her back as she arched and moaned. Again and again. Back and forth. Every touch of his mouth went straight to her sex and made her hotter.

Finally, he allowed her to sit up. He tumbled her to her

back and wedged his large body between her aching thighs. He looked rumpled and wild and sexy as hell. He kissed her hard, his tongue claiming her mouth with ruthless intent.

He withdrew his cock almost completely. She gripped his forearms. "Please."

A lock of his hair fell across his forehead. "Please what?"

She pouted. "You know what I want."

Sweat dampened his chest. His face reflected the toll it was taking to hold back. "The fantasy or the reality?" He ground out the question as he eased away an inch farther.

For one panicked second she imagined he might leave her like this. Aching. Hungry. Needy.

She wrapped her feet around his calves, arching her back and keeping their bodies barely touching. "You, Trey. Only you."

He shoved deep without warning, filling her so completely that it triggered her climax and his own. They held each other through the raging storm of release, and then they tumbled into a deep, exhausted sleep, locked in each other's arms.

Five

$\mathcal{G}$ina surfaced to the sight of Trey pulling on his damp swim trunks. She reared up on one elbow, her thoughts fuzzy after a brief nap. "Where are you going?" It was difficult to read his expression, even though the faint light of dawn was beginning to creep into the cabin.

He shrugged into his shirt and shoes, turning away from her as he scooped up his room key. "Go back to sleep, sweetheart. I'm going to head back to my cabin and clean up and change. I'll meet you at nine in the dining room for breakfast."

He bent over the bed and pressed a gentle kiss to her lips. "Sweet dreams." He was gone before she had a chance to respond.

She lay there for a few minutes feeling groggy. In the silence, she heard heavy rain lashing the one window. And in the distance, the crack of thunder. The ship seemed to be listing and swaying like a drunken sailor.

Too bad. They were supposed to dock this morning at

the cruise line's private island. It would have been nice to snuggle under a beach umbrella with Trey all day and enjoy the sand and the sunshine. But apparently, that wasn't in the cards.

On the other hand, there was something to be said for spending a rainy afternoon in bed. With a smile on her lips and an unfamiliar warmth in her heart, she snuggled deeper into her comfy feather pillow and settled back to sleep.

Trey was late for breakfast. Gina glanced at her watch and frowned. He was punctual normally. That hadn't changed in the years she had known him. It was difficult to rise to the position of responsibility he held without being disciplined.

She ordered toast and coffee and chatted with her fellow passengers, assuring herself he would step through the doorway any minute. He'd expended a lot of calories last night. Surely he was starving.

At nine fifteen she was pissed. At nine thirty she was worried. At a quarter till ten, she was embarrassed when the waiter offered her one last cup of coffee. The dining room had emptied for the most part, and she sat alone at a table for eight . . . waiting.

She shook her head. "No thanks."

She stood up and walked outside, feeling hurt and angry. She concentrated on the anger. It was easier than contemplating what she had done.

She had fulfilled her pact with Catherine and Kallie. She had participated in a naughty one-night stand with a handsome stranger. Well, okay . . . she had fudged on the stranger part. But not entirely. She certainly couldn't claim to know the inner workings of Trey Lipman's mind. Just because last night was the most beautiful and amazing and fulfilling sexual experience of her life didn't mean he felt the same.

She'd thrown herself at him . . . for the second time in their acquaintance . . . and this time he had taken her up on it.

She stood under an overhang and watched the angry sea. The tumultuous waves would have scared her to death yesterday. But now she knew there was something more frightening than the fathomless ocean in the midst of a storm. Now she knew real fear. She'd offered up her heart, unasked, and it was in danger of being dashed to bits on the rocks of Trey's indifference.

In her mind, she assessed and discarded possibilities. To her knowledge, he had spent the entire day before without his cell phone or his computer. It was possible that once he returned to his cabin he'd been caught up in some kind of business crisis.

But even still. He could have called. Or sent a note to the dining room.

Maybe he was already regretting their lovemaking. Maybe he thought she would be clingy and demanding and had misread his male lust for something more. It wouldn't be unusual behavior for a thirty-nine-year-old bachelor.

Perhaps he intended to avoid her for the remainder of

the cruise. Fine. Let him. She would simply ignore him. Perhaps flirt with that nice Mr. Pelley, the retired appliance salesman. He wasn't a day over sixty-five, and he had all his own teeth.

She went back to her room and changed into jeans and a T-shirt, topping the casual outfit with a thin hooded raincoat. She put on socks and tennis shoes, tucked her hair up, and went outside.

The turbulent weather suited her mood perfectly. She paced from one deck to the next, relishing the rain on her face, immune to the chill in the air. And still she vacillated between deep hurt, hot anger, and anxious concern.

Once she even stopped by her cabin to see if there were any messages. And then she was mad at herself when, of course, there weren't.

So she walked some more.

Gradually, aided by the brisk exercise and the chance to really think instead of just react, she gained a measure of peace. She'd spent a lot of years with her self-esteem in the toilet, but it was dumb to let a knee-jerk response make her second-guess herself again.

Trey couldn't have faked his feelings last night. He'd been tender and sweet and hotly passionate. No way had he simply written her off as another conquest. It didn't make sense. It didn't add up.

Something must have happened.

When she knocked at Trey's door and got no response, she found a steward and asked to be let into Trey's room. It was no real surprise when the man declined, but she was desperate. She did the whole bat-your-eyes-smile-sweetly thing and convinced the guy to at least see if Trey was there.

She hovered in the corridor as the uniformed man tapped sharply at the door, used his key, and entered. She could barely hear traces of a murmured conversation and then the steward reappeared.

He smiled briefly and impersonally. "You can go on in, ma'am."

She stepped into the gloomy room with her heart pounding. The curtains were pulled shut, the lights were out, and Trey was nowhere to be seen.

But there was a large lump under the covers on the bed, and when a muffled groan that sounded distinctly masculine echoed in the small room, she knew she had located her quarry.

"Trey?" She stepped forward anxiously.

He didn't respond, and her pulse skipped a beat. She approached the bed and sat gingerly on the side. Her hand touched what she thought might be a shoulder.

The lump moved. "Go away."

Now she frowned. Even with his voice muffled, she could hear the misery in his blunt words.

Slowly, she peeled back the covers. He winced and flung an arm over his face. He rolled to his back, groaning. His chest was bare, and he wore a pair of pale blue cotton boxers.

His hair was spiked and messy, and his face was an

interesting shade of green. She didn't know skin could turn that color. She moved his arm so she could see his eyes. They were sunken and underscored with dark circles. It was hard to believe this was the same man who had screwed her so wildly and energetically just a few hours before.

She laid her hand on his forehead, checking to see if he had a fever. "What's wrong, Trey?"

He opened one bloodshot eye and glared at her. "I'm seasick."

Her mouth dropped open as everything suddenly made sense. The storm had started in the middle of the night. Trey hadn't left her bed to shower and dress. He had crawled back here to hide.

Despite her sympathy for his obvious suffering, she was forced to smother a grin. She bit down on her lower lip. "Have you—?"

"Thrown up?" He snarled the words at her.

She winced at his hostility. Sick males were often surly. "Yeah. That's what I was asking."

He tugged the sheet back to his chin. "No. But god knows I've tried."

"Do you have medicine?"

"They brought me something an hour ago."

"Is it helping?"

"Maybe. I don't know. I can't tell."

She stroked his arm. "If it makes you feel any better, it looked like the storm was beginning to break up when I came in a few minutes ago. They are already starting to post signs that say we may be able to dock at the island after all."

"Oh, goody."

Now she did smile. Seeing the normally unflappable Trey Lipman grumpy and vulnerable did something to her heart. Every maternal instinct she hadn't known she possessed came rushing to the fore. She tapped his hip. "Move over."

She shed everything down to her panties and bra and climbed in beside him. She pulled him into her embrace spoon fashion and wrapped her arms around his waist. His skin radiated heat that warmed her chilled body.

A deep sigh shuddered though his chest, and he clasped one of her hands in his. "Feels wonderful," he mumbled sleepily. "I'm sorry I didn't send you a message. I wasn't thinking straight."

She kissed his spine. "Don't worry about it. Try to get some rest."

Trey jerked awake with a start, disoriented and dizzy. He glanced at the clock. He and Gina had slept for a couple of hours. He felt two plump, warm tits crushed against his back and, on further examination, realized that two slender, smooth legs were tangled with his. The arms wrapped around his waist were familiar.

It all came back to him, every embarrassing, humiliating moment. Some stud he was.

He took stock of his surroundings, listening to Gina's even breathing. He was pretty sure he saw a tiny shaft of sunlight sneaking beneath the curtain, and as far as he could tell, the boat was stationary.

Thank god.

Gina must have sensed his wakefulness, because he felt her tongue lick his spine. He shuddered. Her hands played with his nipples. He went hard in less time than it took a choir to shout hallelujah.

She nuzzled the back of his neck. "How's your stomach?"

He paused to consider. "No problems."

"And your head?"

"Fine." He was feeling better by the minute. "Did you have a reason in particular for asking, or were you simply being solicitous of my health?"

Her hands were trespassing just about everywhere. She bit his shoulder, inexplicably sending zings of fire to his cock. Who knew they were connected?

He heard the smile in her voice. "Well, I've been told I'm a caring person. It's possible that I'm merely being empathetic."

"But not probable."

She chuckled, stroking his prick in ways that made his legs weak even though he was lying down. "I would have to say you're right. Have I told you how much I enjoyed our swim last night?"

"That's all?" His masculine pride wanted to hear the full marks.

He felt her shrug. "There were other moments that were entertaining."

"Entertaining?" That was almost insulting. He'd done some of his best work last night.

"Okay, then . . . awesome, earth-shaking, off-the-charts orgasmic."

He smiled, feeling like a very lucky man. "That's more like it."

She circled the head of his cock with her thumb and forefinger, squeezing gently. "Are you sure you're feeling better?"

He shuddered, too damn close to exploding already. "Hell, yes."

"Would it be terribly insensitive of me to ask you to make love to me again?"

He gasped when her hands moved to cup his balls. He trembled like a girl and laughed roughly, breaking free of her embrace and rolling her to her back with him on top. But he didn't join their bodies, not yet.

He looked down at her, his chest tight. "How do you feel about big church weddings?"

Her eyes widened, and a trace of vulnerability shadowed her face. Her lips twisted in a self-deprecating smile. Her tone was flip, though her expression was guarded. "For other people? They're great. For me? I'd rather swim naked in a shark-infested pool."

He leaned on one arm and, with his free hand, traced her lips. Her lovely, begging-to-be-kissed lips. He stared down into her sea green eyes, ready to drown willingly in their depths. "Marry me, Gina. Today. On the beach. We'll get the ship's captain to perform the ceremony."

For once she was speechless. He decided he should

savor the moment. His feisty, razor-tongued beauty was rarely at a loss for words.

He played with a nipple, watching it furl and harden. "Gina?"

She shuddered, from his proposal or from his touch, he couldn't tell. "Kallie and Catherine would kill me."

"Do you care?" He shifted his attention to the other breast.

She closed her eyes, panting in short, ragged breaths. "I haven't heard you mention love."

Shit. He'd screwed up the order here. She shouldn't have to beg. "I do love you," he muttered. "With all my heart. I've loved you one way or another for most of my life, I think."

He tested her readiness with a finger, teasing the folds of her sex and slicking moisture around her clit. He centered his cock and entered her tight passage an inch. He stopped, his chest heaving. "A response might be nice, my love. To any of the above. I've waited a helluva long time to say those words."

Her eyes were shiny with tears, her smile tentative but softly radiant. "I love you, Trey Lipman. I never stopped. And yes . . . I will marry you."

He flexed his hips and drove deep. They both gasped. He leaned forward on his elbows, kissing her tenderly. "I want babies," he muttered.

She wrapped her legs around his waist, arching her back and giving him another half inch. "Yes."

"And a long, long, romantic honeymoon. On dry ground."

She nibbled his lips like an erotic piranha. "Whatever you say, my sweet. I'm not overly fond of the water myself. But we have two more nights on board this damned ship."

He groaned. "Don't remind me." He rotated his hips, smiling fiercely when she cried out. "We'll just have to tough it out."

Her head thrashed from side to side, her fiery hair spread over his pillow. He slid out and entered her again with a deliberately lazy stroke.

"Trey." Gina's ragged cry increased his hunger. How had he lived without her for so long? How had he been so blind to the hole in his life?

His control frayed, and he thrust quickly, no longer capable of finesse. "Come for me, Gina," he demanded. Hunger blinded him. He pinched her ass as he ground his shaft against her clit. And as her lovely, warm body crested in a beautiful climax, he emptied his seed deep against the mouth of her womb and counted the moments until he could do it again.

Four hours later Trey Lipman and Gina McCutcheon faced each other on a quiet beach, backlit by a spectacular sunset, and became husband and wife. She wore a familiar white dress. He wore an elegant tux. They were both barefoot.

The ceremony was traditional, though the setting was

not. He grinned cockily when she promised to love and obey. She smiled wickedly, promising interesting retribution.

The officiant blessed a college ring wrapped with about a pound of tape to keep it from sliding off the bride's slender finger.

A few interested passengers cheered when the captain pronounced Gina and Trey husband and wife. Most people were already on board getting ready for dinner.

When the hoopla was over, everyone disappeared with smiles and congratulatory waves, leaving the newlyweds to stand alone at the edge of the water.

Trey took his wife's hand, feeling his heart stumble. He knew there had never been a more beautiful bride.

She linked her arms around his waist as he gathered her close. He nuzzled her hair. She had worn it loose, and some kind person had provided a gardenia to tuck behind her ear. He sighed, feeling at peace and hungry at the same time. It was an odd dichotomy of emotions, but he decided he liked it.

Gina toyed with the buttons on his vest. "I checked the weather forecast. The skies are supposed to be clear until we get back home."

Trey chuckled. "That's a relief. But just in case, I think we might need to stay close to my bed."

She nipped his chin with sharp white teeth. "Our bed."

"I stand corrected." He grasped a handful of curls and pulled her head back so he could reach her lips. A man should be able to kiss his wife on their wedding day with gentle reverence. Apparently, he had a lot to learn about being a sensitive male.

Need clawed in his belly as fiery arousal tightened his loins and weakened his knees. His mouth covered hers in ravenous passes, plundering the sweet taste of her, stealing her breath and his.

They pulled apart, panting. He glanced at his watch. "As appealing as it is to imagine being stranded here with you, I'm pretty sure the reality wouldn't be all that romantic."

"You don't think they would leave us, do you?"

"I'd rather not put it to the test."

He took her hand, leading her across the sand. As they walked slowly back to the other side of the island where the large ship lay waiting just offshore, a crewman in a small launch beckoned them with a wave.

Trey looked down at their two sets of footsteps. Side-by-side. Large and small. Together. Forever.

He bent his head and whispered what he planned to do to her when they were back on the boat. Gina's expressive face flushed and then paled. Her lips trembled. "Is it wrong to be so happy?" she whispered. "I don't deserve you. I don't deserve this."

He took her hand in his, twining his fingers with hers. "Nobody *deserves* happiness, sweetheart. But sometimes, when we're very lucky, it finds *us*. You and I were meant to be together. For better or worse. It's not about being entitled to anything. It's about loving each other and sharing that love with the people we care about. The people who need it."

He lifted her hand and kissed her fingers. "Come on, Mrs. Lipman. We have a ship to catch."

And then he bundled her up in his arms and strode with her over the threshold of their new life.

Epilogue

At a simple wrought-iron table in the garden of one of Charleston's finest restaurants, three beautiful women each lifted a glass of champagne.

Gina, her face pinched and white, set hers down quickly and dashed for the bathroom. When she returned several minutes later, her friends gave her sympathetic but envious smiles.

Catherine wrinkled her nose. "I know you weren't really going to drink it, but I thought you'd at least be able to *simulate* a toast."

Gina, her face pale but her expression smug, grinned complacently. "I can do this." The three flutes were lifted in the air a second time.

Catherine sighed happily as she gently touched glasses with her friends. "To our little mother-to-be, Gina . . . and to Trey, who didn't waste a bit of time."

Catherine and Kallie laughed as Gina blushed. It was unusual but heartwarming to see their sometimes cynical friend so happy. "To Gina."

Gina pressed a hand to her flat stomach, still clearly amazed that life was growing there—a daughter or a son who would be reared with love and care and attention. "Thank you. It doesn't seem quite real yet." Then she smirked. "But if you both hadn't been set on fancy society weddings, *you* could be pregnant already."

Kallie shook her head. "Beau still gets queasy even thinking about fatherhood. I'm sure I'll be able to ease him into the whole idea eventually. As long as we're in bed, I can get him to agree to almost anything."

Gina chuckled. "And what about you, Catherine? After all, you got a jump start on *both* of us. You could already be a mama by now if you'd wanted to."

Catherine smiled wistfully. "Don't think we haven't talked about it. But Phillip's work still takes him abroad quite a bit. I want to travel with him for now, and later he has plans to rearrange some things so that he can be here in Charleston for the most part."

The waiter brought out a small iced birthday cake with three lit candles. The trio of women leaned forward and blew them out, laughing softly when the flames were extinguished in unison.

Gina lifted her glass again. "To naughty fantasies fulfilled . . . to weddings and babies. May June get here quickly."

Kallie was solemn, but she had a twinkle in her eye. "To the men in our lives—hot, handsome hunks every one. We are truly blessed."

Catherine completed the round of toasts. "And to

friends who make us brave enough to reach for what we want."

"Or who," Kallie giggled.

Gina smiled dreamily. "If I'd known it was possible to have sex this amazing, I would have become a slut much sooner."

Catherine grinned, knowing her friend far too well to believe that. "It was Trey who tapped into your inner vixen. And every time I see him, he looks pretty darned proud of knocking you up so quickly."

Gina leaned forward, her expression urgent and determined. "We should meet back here in twenty years exactly."

Kallie tucked a bare foot beneath her skirt. "To see where our fantasies have taken us?"

Gina nodded. Catherine nodded. "Of course," they said in unison.

A couple of miles offshore, a small white yacht cut through the murky blue-green water, its sleek hull gleaming brightly in the midday sun. Up on top, the owner of the vessel stood confidently at the helm. His cotton shirt and khaki shorts were more casual than his normal dress. On his wrist a thin gold watch kept track of at least five time zones.

With one hand on the wheel, he glanced back at his passengers. Beau Donovan sprawled on the starboard seat with one knee propped up and a beer dangling from the fingers of his left hand. At his feet sat a large cooler ready for lunch, stocked full of boiled shrimp and the requisite side dishes, all compliments of Beau's restaurant.

On the port-side seat, Trey Lipman sat, spine erect, gazing pensively out to sea. If his grip on the railing was a bit white-knuckled, neither of his companions was rude enough to mention it.

Phillip returned his attention to the horizon and spoke casually. "You okay back there, Trey?" Catherine would never forgive him if he didn't look after Gina's new hubby, especially with a baby on the way.

The quiet, intense man's smile was a tad strained. "I took Dramamine. I may fall asleep on you, but other than that, I'm fine."

The three women in their lives had insisted on this after-the-fact quasi–bachelor party in Trey's honor. Phillip had been charged with providing the entertainment, and Beau the food. Phillip suspected that Trey might have enjoyed a land-based outing more, but the females, even Gina, who wasn't too fond of the water herself, had seemed oblivious to Trey's lukewarm reception of the idea.

Phillip adjusted his speed and locked the wheel long enough to reach into the cooler for a bottle of water. Beau seemed to be dozing behind his reflective sunglasses, his head resting against the rail, so Phillip took the opportunity to extend his acquaintance with the second man who would be a significant part of his life. With their trio of wives closer than most sisters, it was inevitable.

He returned to the wheel and took a long slug of water. Trey held a beer but didn't appear to be drinking it. Fortunately, the wind today was almost nonexistent, and the chop was minimal.

Phillip cocked his head. "Come join me. Take a turn at the wheel."

Trey's expression was at first taken aback and then intrigued. He set his bottle in a beverage holder and rose to his feet.

Phillip stepped aside. "There's nothing to it on a day like today. Just keep those two marks lined up and we'll be steady on our course."

Trey placed his hands on the wheel, and in moments his face changed. Phillip knew he was feeling the powerful thrum of the engine and the insistent tug as the water wrestled with the boat for supremacy.

Phillip grinned inwardly. He'd bet money that Trey would be hooked before the day was out. He finished his water and tucked the empty plastic bottle in a recycle bag. "I've got to tell you, Trey. I was pretty damn jealous when Catherine told me you and Gina were expecting."

Trey's cocky grin was entirely justified in Phillip's opinion. The other man's engaging happiness took five years off his solemn face. "I'm so goddammed excited, it's embarrassing," he said quietly.

Phillip shrugged. "You're entitled." He sighed, stretching his arms above his head for a moment, relishing the crisp ocean breeze in his face. "I haven't told Catherine yet—I've been saving it for a surprise—but I've just hired a new man to oversee all my European interests. I'll still have to travel some, but only a couple of times a year. If Catherine's willing, we won't be far behind you and Gina in the baby race."

Trey's brief nod and briefer response spoke volumes. "Smart man."

Beau joined them at the rail, his sunglasses tucked in his pocket. The alert interest in his blue eyes gave lie to his earlier drowsiness. "Don't count me out, guys. Kallie is still wrapped up in getting her art career established, but my job has a lot of flexibility. I'd love to start a family, the sooner the better. And let's face it. If Catherine and Gina were *both* pregnant, you know my little Kallie would feel left out."

Phillip chuckled. "True. They've spent their lives doing everything together. Why stop now?"

Beau leaned over the rail to grin at the dolphins gamboling in the boat's frothy wake. "I'm going to ease her into the idea," he said over his shoulder, his smile confident.

Phillip laughed. "Shouldn't be too difficult." He paused, and then asked the question that had been on his mind all morning. "So, I'm guessing that you both know about the challenge they made to each other?"

Beau straightened, and he and Trey nodded, not even bothering to conceal their grins.

"Yep," Beau said.

"Ditto." Trey's reply was accompanied by a smirk.

Phillip shook his head. "We're going to have to band together, my friends. Those women are extremely smart and too damned sexy for their own good."

Trey chuckled quietly. "Are you complaining?"

Beau snorted. "Not me. I know when I've got a good thing going."

Phillip held up his hands. "Hey, I'm not crazy. Life's just

about perfect at the moment. But I can't help wondering about the future. They have the power to gang up on us any time they choose."

Trey shrugged. "Three on three. I'll take those odds."

Beau's brows narrowed, suddenly getting Phillip's drift. "You're wondering if they might cook up another fantasy wager . . . right?"

Trey whistled, his expression arrested. "I'm with you now. We'd be putty in their hands."

"Or something harder," Beau deadpanned.

Male laughter rose over the rumble of the engine, disappearing into the sunlit clouds above. And despite Phillip's words of caution, none of the three appeared unduly concerned about his fate.

Champagne flowed a final time. "To twenty years," Catherine said softly, her face alight with happiness.

"Of living and loving and laughing," Kallie added.

"Make that fifty," Gina muttered weakly, dabbing at her forehead with a damp napkin.

And of all the toasts ever made in that particular spot in that particular city, it was the most deeply felt and the most passionately executed.

If you love sensual stories like *Play with Me*,
then look for Janice Maynard's next sexy romp . . .

IMPROPER ETIQUETTE

On sale July 2007

Read on for a sneak peek. . . .

I must be candid, dear friends. . . . We live in a man's world. But an intelligent and resourceful female can gently lead the male of the species in a desired direction. Men are simple creatures. Their needs are few: food, physical intimacy, and the opportunity to conquer. Keeping these realities in mind, I have put together a volume of advice that may well be invaluable for today's young woman searching for a mate. Follow my instructions (though they might make you blush), and soon you will be able to add that lovely appellation "Mrs." to the front of your name. Good luck and happy hunting. . . .

—Excerpted from *Miss Matilda's Guide to Love and Romance for the Proper Young Lady*, copyright 1949

*G*ood manners were good manners, plain and simple. Southern girls learned that from the cradle and ignored it at their peril. If the gentleman living next door had been eighty-five, deaf as a post, and crotchety, Francesca Fremont *still* would have taken him a plate of homemade dessert. But the fact that her new neighbor was well over six feet tall and fiercely gorgeous made the whole "welcome to town" overture much more fun and intriguing.

She smoothed plastic wrap over the mound of freshly baked cinnamon rolls and eyed the plate with satisfaction. It was part of her grandmother's wedding china, and she had even added a lacy paper doily that nicely accented the old-fashioned floral pattern.

Some people might balk at the idea of using heirloom dishes for such a purpose, but Francesca was a firm believer in the "use it or lose it" philosophy. Lovely things shouldn't be tucked away in drawers and cabinets. They deserved to be used and appreciated every day.

She set the plate on the table and dashed to her bedroom for a quick peek in the mirror. When she was baking, she tended to ignore her appearance, and today she wanted to look presentable. Not that her faded denim jeans and yellow tank top were going to win any fashion awards, but at least they weren't splotched with flour.

Her face was flushed from the heat in the kitchen. Her old window-unit air-conditioner wasn't very reliable, and most of the time she had to resort to opening up the house— at least the rooms that had functional screens—and relying on ceiling fans for circulation. She slicked a bit of gloss over her lips and ran a brush through her hair. That would have to do.

She retrieved the plate of goodies and set off across the yard. The piquant scent of honeysuckle hung on the early morning breeze. There wasn't a cloud in the sky, and the earth seemed verdant and teeming with life. The temperature was pleasant now, but by midafternoon the heat would be scorching.

Her property and her neighbor's had once upon a time been a small farm. Back in the 1930s, the old farmer had split the land right down the middle and given half to his son and new daughter-in-law.

Out at the road, the entrances to the two long, winding driveways were at least a quarter of a mile apart, but the two homesteads actually sat quite close together near the middle of the original plot. They were separated by a large, mature screen of English boxwoods, but a narrow well-worn rut in the dirt between two sections attested to the fact that the families had visited back and forth frequently.

Sadly, the young couple had apparently been unable to have children. In the late eighties, with no more descendants in line to inherit, the property began to change hands, and Francesca had been lucky enough to buy her portion several years back.

She slipped through the hedge and stopped abruptly. The neglected, run-down house, its design a mirror image of her own, was as dilapidated as ever, but its dismal appearance barely merited a glance. Her attention was firmly focused on the new homeowner, who at the moment was perched atop a rickety wooden ladder, cleaning out his gutters.

He was bare from the waist up, and the muscles in his arms and chest flexed and rippled as he worked, making her knees weak. His iPod was tucked into his back pocket, and the jeans he had on looked as if they had come straight from the department store. There was still a crease in the crisp, dark denim.

For some reason she doubted he was the kind of man who usually did his own home maintenance. Not that he wasn't capable. He was physically imposing, his masculine strength and power clearly evident. But she'd encountered him in town two days before, and she was pretty sure that the man she'd seen at the bank was the real persona.

That day, he'd been wearing a suit that probably cost more than her eight-year-old car, and it didn't take the New York plates on his Lexus and his clipped New England accent to convince her that he didn't belong in Camron, Tennessee. It was like seeing a shark in a freshwater creek. It just didn't add up.

Camron was only forty-five minutes from Knoxville, a university city with cultural opportunities and shopping and entertainment. But despite that proximity, her sleepy little town was decidedly rural. Everyone knew his or her neighbors, and newcomers were automatically suspect, particularly if they hailed from north of the Mason-Dixon Line.

If this man planned to stick around, he'd have to develop a thick skin. He was clearly a fish out of water. And since she was his closest neighbor, it was up to her to ensure that he felt welcome.

She cleared her throat. "Good morning."

He didn't acknowledge her presence, and she realized that with earplugs in place he couldn't hear her over his music. She sighed, feeling self-conscious. In spite of herself, her gaze drifted to his taut butt. It would be a yummy handful for a woman intent on carnal pursuits. She hadn't seen a nicer one in longer than she cared to remember.

Good gravy. She had to get a handle on her hormones. At the moment, she was reluctantly (and, please God, temporarily) celibate. Which made it difficult to view her neighbor with dispassionate courtesy.

She noted with appreciation his sculpted features and strong nose. His dark hair gleamed black as shiny coal in the morning sun, and his olive-toned skin was naturally tanned. Despite her Italian-sounding name, Francesca had inherited her Scottish ancestors' fair skin, blue eyes, and strawberry blond hair. She was envious of his ability to labor in the blazing sun with impunity.

The paragon of male beauty continued working, his broad, long-fingered hands covered in black muck. They were big hands, and they moved purposefully. She tried again, a little louder. "Good morning." When that produced no results, she yelled. *"Good morning!"*

As soon as the words left her mouth, she realized her mistake. He jerked in shock as her greeting finally pierced his music-induced deafness, and as he did, the ladder tipped backwards. He grabbed for the edge of the roof and got a grip, but the ancient gutter pulled loose with an agonizing screech, and he tumbled several feet into the wildly out-of-control rosebushes below.

Francesca darted forward and then froze as a stream of truly impressive profanity emanated from the still-quivering greenery. She knew from experience that the thorns were lethal, and she winced in sympathy as he struggled to his feet.

When he finally stood up, his scowl was black enough to send a brave man scurrying, but her shaking legs didn't seem to be getting the message from her brain.

"I am *so* sorry," she whispered, her stomach in a knot. The skin of his beautiful chest was covered with scratches that oozed blood. His jaw was granite, his piercing eyes shards of obsidian. She clutched the plate to her chest as though expecting to be protected from his wrath by carbs and sugar. She swallowed hard, her throat dry. "I didn't mean to startle you."

She saw his chest rise and fall as he inhaled and expelled a mighty breath. He started to rake the hair from his forehead and stopped abruptly, realizing that his hands were filthy. After a visible effort to control his temper, he spoke with remarkable control. "May I help you?"

She licked her lips, her heart pounding in her chest. "I'm your neighbor, Francesca Fremont. I brought you some sticky buns."

His lips quirked, and for a moment she thought she saw a lick of humor cross his stoic face. But it was gone in an instant, and his eyes narrowed. "Sticky buns?"

She nodded jerkily like one of those silly bobble-head dogs you see on people's dashboards. "Yes. They're homemade. And still warm. I think," she amended hastily. With all the hullabaloo, she wasn't sure exactly how long she'd been standing there.

She held out the plate. "Welcome to Camron." It was a far briefer greeting than she had intended, but she'd totally lost her train of thought.

Still he made no move to take the food from her. Her arms began to get tired, and she felt ridiculously humiliated, even though he'd been the one to tumble in an undignified heap into the bushes.

When she was embarrassed, she tended to get mad. She frowned. "It's dessert, not a bomb." She was going for sarcasm, but he didn't appear to notice. In fact, he seemed to be ignoring her as much as possible.

He looked back up at the roof, where the gutter now hung drunkenly. He sighed, and it wasn't a pleasant sound, not at all. His arms hung by his sides. She had no trouble gathering from his expression that he was anxious to get inside and clean up the blood and the grime. His impatience was a living, breathing entity.

She scuttled forward and laid the plate at his feet, like a clumsy geisha. "They're good," she insisted, beginning to panic at his overly long silence. "And the calories shouldn't matter to you. You could stand to gain a few pounds. Not that you don't look good. You do, of course. Really good. Not that I'm looking . . . I just meant it in a general, healthy way."

Now he looked poleaxed, as though he'd come face-to-face with a rabid bobcat and didn't know quite what to do. She felt her face redden as heat crept up her neck.

She wrapped her arms around her waist. "I'll go now. Let you get back to work. Sorry again."

She backed toward the hedge, and finally he spoke. At the bank two days before, she'd heard him murmur no more than a couple of terse sentences to the teller.

Now, face-to-face, his voice slid over her raw nerves like a deep, rich bass sonata. "Wait."

She sensed his reluctance. Saw it on his face.

He sighed again. "I appreciate the gesture," he said with careful formality. "But I should tell you that I came here to be alone. I won't be socializing. I hope you understand."

She gazed at him blankly as the carefully worded rebuff sank in. Then her poor cheeks flamed even hotter. Wow. Rejection via Emily Post. His careful enunciation and courtesy almost took the sting out of the content. Almost, but not quite.

She lifted her chin. Most people were delighted to get a culinary gift from Francesca. Clearly he wasn't one of them. But damned if she was going to retrieve her offering. She'd give up one of her grandmother's precious plates permanently before she would ever set foot through that darned hedge again.

She turned to walk away, quite unable to think of a suitable response. Then she stopped. The devil should have a name. She managed to meet his impassive gaze, but it took guts. "Around here it's polite to reciprocate when someone introduces herself."

His jaw tightened a fraction more, and for the briefest second she could have sworn she saw pain in his eyes. "Brett Gilman," he said, the three syllables clipped and cold.

She frowned, trying to remember why that sounded familiar.

His scowl returned with a vengeance. "Feel free to Google me," he growled. "I'm sure you'll find out everything you need to know."

———

Brett watched his pretty neighbor escape through the hedge, and he let rip with another string of heartfelt oaths. Would it ever end? He'd come to the backwoods of Tennessee to get away from all the hell he'd endured for the past six months, and from the look on Francesca's face, even Tennessee wasn't far enough removed from New York to protect his secrets. The information age was a bitch.

He'd acted like a jerk, so she wouldn't be too surprised when she read about his sins on the Internet. His life was an open book, and the pages had been sullied, perhaps beyond repair.

He tried to shake off his gloomy thoughts and, instead of dwelling on the past, bent to pick up the plate. Though he sure as hell wasn't an expert, it looked like real bone china. He held the edges carefully, grimacing at his filthy hands, and went inside. The smell of cinnamon made his stomach clench in sharp hunger. He'd found to his dismay that, except for Paul's Pizza Parlor, takeout was nonexistent in Camron. If he had a craving for potstickers at one in the morning, he was out of luck. Other than a tiny diner, the Kentucky Fried Chicken franchise was about the only game in town when it came to restaurants.

Also conspicuous in their absence were Starbucks, any kind of public transportation, liquor stores, fitness centers, and major newspapers. He should count himself lucky that the cable company had finally (only six months ago, he'd been told) run the line out his road, or he'd be stuck with dial-up Internet, for godsakes.

He'd been born and bred in Philadelphia, attended college at Harvard, and moved to New York City at the ripe old age of twenty-two. At thirty-nine, he felt almost like a native. He missed his adopted city already, but he had to admit that the charms of the country were growing on him, not the least of which was the sexy, attractive woman who stopped by uninvited to bring him food from the gods.

He washed his hands, poured himself a glass of cold milk, and gobbled down three cinnamon rolls without blinking. They were almost better than sex. He couldn't cook worth a damn, and if he didn't figure out something soon, he'd be stuck eating peanut butter sandwiches and tasteless frozen dinners indefinitely.

He carefully tucked the plastic wrap around the remaining cinnamon rolls and trudged back outside. The amount of work facing him was daunting, but he welcomed the physical labor. Every drop of sweat seemed cleansing somehow, obliterating even for one small moment in time the memories that kept him awake at night.

He'd purchased the property for an embarrassingly low price, but he'd vastly underestimated the repairs that needed to be made. Though the bungalow-style house was structurally sound, it hadn't received any TLC in years. The loquacious realtor was eager to share the property's history and pointed out that since the last of the original owner's family died in the late eighties, no buyer afterwards had stayed longer than a year or two.

Brett was waiting for a tale about ghosts or similar nonsense, but in reality, most had bought the property with the romantic idea of renovating it, and then when their enthusiasm faded and their pockets emptied, they moved on. It was a money pit.

Brett didn't care. He had money to burn and nowhere he needed to be. He'd found out in a brutal wake-up call that his true friends could be counted on one hand. As an only child, he had no siblings to stand behind him, and his aging parents were too fragile to lend support, even if he'd asked. So here he was, tucked away in a little corner of the South, not exactly starting over, but perhaps hiding out. It was a hell of a thing for a man to admit.

He had no clue what the upcoming months would bring. He was emotionally and physically at the end of his rope, and if he couldn't find healing and hope here in the shadow of the ancient Smoky Mountains, then they probably didn't exist. At least not for him.

He picked up a hammer and a handful of nails, and repositioned the ladder. He had a gutter to fix.

Francesca stared at the computer screen with her stomach churning and her heart crying out in sympathy for the man next door. Now she knew why his name had sounded familiar. MSNBC and CNN had made him a household word, every bit as much as the Enron principals. Brett Gilman had been indicted on a series of nasty white-collar charges, put through a very public and brutal trial, and ultimately exonerated of every offense. The only reason the legal proceedings hadn't dragged on any longer was that the culprit, at his wife's urging, had finally made a full confession and put an end to the media circus. Financial restitution would be made a bit at a time, and Brett's partner and best friend was now facing five to ten years in a minimum-security prison.

No wonder her new neighbor's personality was as warm and fuzzy as an injured grizzly's. He'd literally been through hell and back. His company handled major real estate deals in Manhattan and the surrounding environs. The company had foundered on the rocks for a while, but was now stable again. So why was Brett Gilman, CEO, hiding out in Cam-ron, Tennessee? It didn't make sense.

She fixed herself scrambled eggs and toast for lunch, and after cleaning up the kitchen, she knelt in the corner to prowl through the medium-sized cardboard box on the floor beside her refrigerator. It had been sitting there for long enough. She'd been to a yard sale a couple of weeks ago and had bought a mixed lot of old cookbooks.

She collected them, and although she would toss out duplicates or any that were too damaged, she usually found at least one or two that were interesting. Pushing disturbing thoughts of Brett Gilman to the back of her mind, she began rifling through the dusty box and separating the wheat from the chaff.

The Joy of Cooking went into the "donate somewhere else" pile. She'd come across dozens of copies of that classic over the years. She was happy to find a first edition of a Ju-lia Child volume she didn't have. And then her gaze landed on a small leather-bound book that didn't look like a cook-book at all. She turned it over curiously and flipped to the title page. *Miss Matilda's Guide to Love and Romance for the Proper Young Lady*—copyright 1949.

Well, this should be a hoot. It was almost sixty years old. She stretched out her legs and leaned back against the wall to read. Several of the suggestions made her giggle, but she stopped laughing when she hit number thirteen—*The way to a man's heart (or to his bed) is through his stomach.*

It wasn't twenty-first-century advice, to say the least, but something about it had the ring of truth. Francesca skimmed a few pages, automatically storing away Miss Matilda's suggestions for later reflection. Would she be taking advantage of a vulnerable male to offer him food and maybe something more?

Then she laughed to herself. Despite Brett's history, he looked like a man who could take care of himself. And besides, good etiquette demanded that she help out a neighbor in need. It was the same code that insisted she deliver a casserole to a grieving family or a full meal to a brand-new mom and dad. Certain things simply made sense. And with Miss Matilda egging her on (probably from beyond the grave), she felt it would only be taking the moral high ground to help Brett out.

If her good manners led to something far more titillating, well . . . Miss Matilda would be proud.

About the Author

Janice Maynard came to writing early in life. When her short story, "The Princess and the Robbers," won a red ribbon in her third-grade school arts fair, Janice was hooked. Since then, she has sold numerous books and novellas. She holds a BA from Emory & Henry College and an MA from East Tennessee State University. In 2002, Janice left a fifteen-year career as an elementary school teacher to pursue writing full-time. *Suite Fantasy,* her first release for NAL, hit number eight on the Barnes & Noble trade romance list.

Janice lives with her husband of thirty-one years in beautiful East Tennessee, and they have two grown daughters who make them proud. She can be reached via e-mail at JESM13@aol.com.